Gloiming Koi

Episode #1 of The Kapahu Series

By

L. D. K. Johnson

Sale of this book without a front cover may be unauthorized. If this book is coverless, it may have been reported to the publisher as "unsold or destroyed" and neither the author nor the publisher may have received payment for it.

Copyright © 2013 by L.D.K Johnson

All rights reserved. No portion of this book may be reproduced in any form without permission from the publisher, except as permitted by U.S. copyright law.

For permissions contact Belen Books, LLC.

This is a work of fiction. Names, characters, businesses, places, events, locales, and incidents are either the products of the author's imagination or used in a fictitious manner. Any resemblance to actual persons, living or dead, or actual events or places, or alien abduction, is purely coincidental.

ISBN: 978-1-959715-10-8

Library of Congress Control Number: **2023931337**

Published by Belen Books, LLC
7901 4th St. N, Ste 300, St. Petersburg, FL. 33702 USA
Belenbookspublishing.com

Edited by Beverly R. Waalewyn
Cover by Belen Media Group

🍀 Printed in the United States of America 🍀

FOR MICHAEL

CHAPTER ONE

"Congratulations, graduates! I wish you all the best of luck in your future endeavors," Dean Winthrop beamed from behind the immaculately polished podium. "Go out there and make us proud!"

Thunderous applause followed as the University of Southern California's graduating class spontaneously threw their black caps into the air... all except one.

"Hey!" A muscular, tanned arm snaked around Ali'ikai Kapahu's, Kai to her friends, waist. "Why are you still holding your cap?" Grayish-blue eyes narrowed suspiciously.

"Umm...well, what happened was—" she began, but suddenly stopped.

Aiden Kaplan shook his sable locks with mock disappointment.

"Kai, Kai, Kai." He turned her away from him, placing her back to his front, the movement securing her against his Adonis-like chest.

A fine mist of perspiration suddenly appeared above her upper lip. Although, she doubted his body heat was enough to make her sweat. No, without a doubt it was their close proximity. He had affected her this way for as long as she could remember, and even though she fought her wicked imaginings, fought them with every fiber of her being, he was her kryptonite, and he was breaking her down.

Unfortunately, Kai could no longer deny the 6'3" point guard, engineering major and all-around hottie, stoked her fire. No matter how tired or cranky she was, one devilish grin or lop-sided, boy-next-door smile could cause her heart to flutter and her nether regions to dampen. *Hell!* That was a lie. It was more like a monsoon.

"We talked about this, Kai," her best friend condemned. "You were supposed to *throw it* as a symbol of escaping our educational bonds."

"I had every intention of throwing the damn thing, but couldn't do it," she revealed as a frustrated sigh escaped her dry lips.

"What are you going to do with it?" his eyes narrowed impishly.

"Keep it," she smiled. "As a memento of how we began adulthood."

She wasn't surprised when Aiden threw his head back and laughed.

"That has got to be the dorkiest thing you've ever said to me." He wiped the tears gathered at the corners of his now sky-blue irises. "And believe me, you've said a lot of dorky things during the past four years."

Since the first day they had met, Kai loved the way Aiden's eyes changed colors according to his mood. Normally, they were grayish-blue resembling the sky right before a thunderstorm. When he was making fun of her, which was often, they became a sky blue so radiant they seemed to be lit from within. On the rare occasion he became angry or upset, those same eyes would transform into a dusky indigo. Fortunately, she had only seen those dark orbs once or twice.

Aiden Kaplan was a laid-back, Southern California dude, who would rather arm wrestle with you than come to blows. He was a gentleman who opened doors, shared his food with anyone who was hungry, volunteered at the local children's hospital as a swim instructor and he had taken care of her since the first day of freshman orientation. Everyone loved him, especially her.

"Thanks, Neanderthal," she teased.

"You're welcome, brat," he added flirtatiously, loving his name spoken from those lips.

"Jerk," she jested, filled with mirth.

Suddenly, Aiden paused.

"Harpy."

"Jock-strap," she hissed, hands now perched on her hips.

"Amazon," his blue eyes narrowed mischievously.

Then he readied himself for what would surely follow.

"Beast!" Kai exclaimed and then pinched him hard.

"Ouch! Damn it, Kai!" Aiden grimaced. "What was that for?"

"I hate it when you call me that," she grumbled low in her throat.

"Call you what?" he asked feigning ignorance.

"You know what," she glared.

"Oh yeah...*Amazon*," he smirked. "Kai, of the Amazons. No, no, Kai, leader of the Amazons. Wait, wait! Kai, Queen of the Amazons."

He was assaulted by another arm numbing pinch followed by a punch to the left shoulder.

"I'm sorry! I'm sorry!" Aiden yelped. "I'll be good! I promise!"

Satisfied for the moment, Kai lowered her hands.

"I'm going to miss you," she whispered so only he could hear.

"I'm going to miss you too."

Softly, he kissed her on the temple then smoothed her curly, ebony strands away from her face. On a deep inhale, he filled his lungs with jasmine and Kai's unique scent. It was intoxicating.

"You're my best friend, no matter how dorky you are."

Her left eyebrow arched as the typical "F-off" expression contorted her otherwise placid features, but before she could utter those words her mother's lyrical Hawaiian accent called from across the crowded floor.

"Kai, we've been looking for you everywhere!"

"*Aloha*, Mama." Kai turned and hugged her warmly. "Papa."

On cue, her father bent and hugged her firmly. His 6'7" stature caused her legs to dangle like a ragged-doll. "We are so proud of you, Kai."

"*Mahalo*," she replied, blushing at the compliment. Aiden felt his chest constrict as he stood admiring her profile, thankful that she couldn't see his sappy expression.

Kai was gorgeous, even though she didn't know it. The native Hawaiian was 5'8", inheriting her height from her dad and had the same exotic amber eyes, but her smile, honey complexion, and raven corkscrew curls came from her mom. She was the epitome of athletic grace meets curvy *Sports Illustrated* swimsuit model.

Against his will, Aiden felt his cock harden beneath the loose-fitting gown.

Holy shit! Not now.

Not here.

Not with her parents nearby.

To his horror, Mrs. Kapahu turned her attention to Aiden.

Oh, dear father!

"Aiden, you look so handsome in your cap and gown." Mrs. Kapahu hugged him tightly. For an older woman of 5'2", maybe 110 pounds soaking wet, her embrace was like a vise. He actually thought his eyeballs might pop out of their sockets. "Don't you think he looks handsome, Kai?"

"Not especially," Kai snorted her mock disapproval.

"Ali'ikai Leilani Kapahu," her mother frowned. "Don't be rude."

"Yes, Mama."

"Yeah, Kai. Don't be rude." Aiden's chiseled cheekbones were turning pink from a lack of oxygen. "Try not to succumb to the insolence you so naturally exude."

He wasn't at all surprised when she shot him the bird behind her mother's back.

❀

"Leilani let the boy go." Her father gently unwound his wife's grip from around Aiden's waist. "He's too skinny to hug like that. You're gonna kill him."

Kai smiled as her mom released Aiden and began smoothing out the wrinkles, she had made on his perfectly pressed black graduation gown. The USC school crest embroidered on the matte material signified the four years of hard work, horrible cafeteria food and long study sessions they had survived.

And even though Kai hated to admit it, Aiden *looked* good…delicious actually, but she would never tell him that. He already had an over-inflated ego. Any more compliments and the man wouldn't be able to exit the auditorium's double doors. For some reason, he looked extremely uncomfortable with her mother's ministrations. *Whatever.* Aiden was…well, Aiden was…*Aiden.*

"I wish your brother could have come to see you graduate," Mr. Kapahu stated solemnly, his amber eyes glistening under the fluorescent lights.

"I know." Kai frowned unable to hide her disappointment. "Koa said he couldn't get leave because of SEAL training." She smiled, but it didn't reach her eyes. "I told him we were recording the whole thing, so he'd see it anyway."

"Well, Aiden." Mr. Kapahu looked around before asking, "Where are your parents?"

Aiden shifted uncomfortably.

"My dad is an admiral in the Navy, and he had some important meetings in Washington, D.C. this weekend, so he couldn't make it."

"What about your mom?" Mrs. Kapahu inquired; concern etched into her lovely features.

"She passed away when I was thirteen," he replied uneasily, clearing his throat.

Kai had known Aiden's mother had died in a car crash leaving him in the sole care of his father. A man who was more concerned with climbing the ranks of the Navy career ladder than spending time with his only child, but Aiden seemed okay with their lack of a relationship, even though she didn't understand it.

Fortunately, she was blessed with a large, supportive family. They took care of each other, ate meals together every Sunday, and never judged anyone without knowing their situation first. It was difficult for her to imagine a father not having much to do with his own flesh and blood.

Growing up in Oahu, her parents had been strict with both her and her older brother, Koa. Their number one rule was: *'No dating before your eighteenth birthday.'* They had successfully run off every boy who'd ever shown her any interest, but for some inexplicable reason, her parents believed Aiden and she belonged together.

"I'm sorry to hear that." Leilani took his hand in hers. "I guess that means you'll have to join us for dinner."

No. No. No.

"He has other plans," Kai misdirected. "Don't you, Aiden?"

"I don't actually." His eyes sparkled mischievously. "But I couldn't possibly intrude."

"It's no intrusion, son." Mr. Kapahu slapped him playfully on the back almost causing him to fall face forward onto the floor. "You like seafood?"

"No, he's allergic to seafood. Aren't you?" Kai silently pleaded.

"In fact, I love seafood," he smirked.

"Don't you remember last year at the Fourth of July picnic you ate a lobster roll and got really sick; broke out in all of those itchy hives?" she frantically fabricated. "Your throat closed up and everything."

"I don't remember that." His eyes narrowed and she knew she was in trouble.

She knew she was in trouble, but she didn't care. There was no way in hell she was going to sit next to the incorrigible, conceited, perfectly-constructed demigod of a man with wet panties all through dinner while he buttered-up her parents; those poor unsuspecting, innocent fools. It was like inviting Jack the Ripper to the red-light district…it would end badly. Of that she was certain.

Kai stepped in front of Aiden in a last-ditch effort.

"Mama, Papa, if he doesn't want to have dinner with us, then don't force him." Kai's eyes were wide. "You should stick with your original plans."

When she realized she had inadvertently thrown down the gauntlet, it was too late. Aiden took that as a challenge.

"Thank you, sir…ma'am. I would love to join your family for dinner."

No!

Kai felt her palms begin to sweat. The look that skinny, blue-eyed freak was giving her made her want to give him another blow, but this punch would be aimed at his more vulnerable parts. Oh, yeah. He was going to get his.

In his usual gentlemanly fashion, Aiden allowed her parents to lead the way out of the crowded room and joined Kai bringing up the rear. Boldly, he placed his right hand on the small of her back, right above her ass and leaned down close to her ear. Her breath hitched as he gently bit the sensitive skin of her earlobe.

"This is going to be so much fun," he informed, haughtily.

"I. Hate. You," Kai growled, wanting to hit him again.

Her statement only made him chuckle.

"I know… I know."

The fraternity house was wall-to-wall people, all of them moving in time to the music, and having a wonderful time. Even the students who normally would not attend house parties were celebrating their last night of college life. It would be a night to remember.

"So, where's your girl?" USC Power forward, Marcus Davis searched the fraternity house living room.

"She's not my girl." Aiden craned his neck trying to find the pain in his ass, affectionately known as Amazon. "I don't know. She'll get here when she gets here."

He glanced down at the platinum *Tag Heuer* watch his father had sent him as a graduation present.

"Where the hell is she?"

"Yeah, she's your girl," Marcus smirked.

"Stop saying that, you—"

"Stop saying what?" Kai playfully punched him in the stomach.

"Nothing," he wheezed, doubled over in pain.

"Hey, hot stuff." Marcus pushed Aiden out of the way and proceeded to embrace her lithe form. "Gimme some sugar."

His *'friend'* turned his face so she could kiss him on the cheek. Shamelessly, Kai looked Aiden directly in the eyes, pushed-up on her tip-toes, and planted a loud kiss on the other man's face. Marcus chuckled then quickly sobered when Aiden's lips thinned in warning, making his friend gently push her arm's length away.

In typical fashion, Kai grabbed the drink out of his hand and tasted.

"Yuck! It's beer." She handed the disposable plastic cup back to her still frowning best friend. "Why are you guys holding up this wall?"

Kai put her hands on her hips and waited for a response, but none came.

"This is meant to be the party to end all parties," she reminded. "The final curtain call, the last man standing."

"Are you high?" Aiden teased while pretending to look at her pupils to make sure they weren't dilated.

"Stop that!" she ordered, smacking his hands away.

The fast-thumping, hip-hop track ended and a slower reggae tune by *Bob Marley* began to play. It was her favorite song.

"Marcus, dance with me."

Aiden shot him an icy glare.

"Hmm...maybe another time, Kai. Hey!" the intelligent graduate cleverly diverted the conversation. "I see a friend of mine over there. I'll see y'all later."

The traitor! Who would have thought a skinny white boy could scare off a rather intimidating black man with just one look.

Nervously, Kai looked around then nudged him with her elbow.

"Would you like to dance?"

Against his will, his errant cock began to harden.

"With you?" he blurted.

"Of course, with me." His best friend gave him one of her heartbreaking, make you want to come-in-your-pants smiles.

"No."

Surprised, she stared at him as if he'd grown a second head, confusion clouding her expressive amber eyes. "I mean...never mind."

He was such a moron!

"Okay," she stated somberly as she turned on her heels and walked over to the bar.

Several of the basketball players, his teammates and second family, greeted her warmly. *Freaking hell!* She looked good enough to eat.

With an appreciative gaze, he examined the strapless black summer dress she'd chosen to wear. The fitted skirt reaching a couple of inches above her knees, accentuating the most exquisitely toned, tanned legs he had ever seen that went on for miles. A simple pair of wedge sandals adorned her feet, hair straightened and pulled back into a high ponytail. A thin silver necklace and matching small hoop earrings finished off the outfit. The only makeup on her flawless skin consisted of a little eyeliner and some lip gloss. She was absolute perfection.

Right now, Aiden was content to watch his island flower as she chatted with friends and hugged and took pictures with people they'd known since the beginning of their college careers. It was nice seeing her out having fun instead of being holed-up in the library or at volleyball practice.

It wasn't surprising that Kai had gotten a full ride to USC with both academic and athletic scholarships. She was the captain of USC's women's volleyball team, graduated Summa Cum Laude with a bachelor's degree in Physical Therapy and was still as down to earth as the day she'd accidentally dropped a physics textbook on his head in the campus bookstore.

Kai was sort of nerdy back then, glasses, braces, really tall, very thin and always wore her hair in a braid. She wore baggy jeans and t-shirts all the time and was painfully shy. However, once you got to know her, she blew you away with her sense of humor and fun-loving nature.

From that day on, they were inseparable. The Hawaiian goddess kept him in line with his studies and didn't put up with any of his shit. She was tough, but fair and always encouraged him to work hard and not rely on his family's money or his father's fame. Kai made him want to be a better man, but with all that, he'd never had the courage to ask her out. In his opinion, she was way out of his league.

So instead, freshman year Aiden went out with anything blonde with questionable morals. Actually, he went for anything in a skirt that would give him the time of day. Unfortunately, his first year of college he had demoted himself to a man-slut or *kolohe*, the Hawaiian word for rascal, as Kai liked to call him.

When he returned to USC the following fall, he met Kai at the airport and his whole world changed. In reality...Kai had changed. She had gotten Lasik surgery and no longer wore glasses. Her braces had come off revealing a perfect Hollywood smile and the once anorexic-looking girl had gained a little over twenty pounds from working at her Uncle Choy's bakery. To his delight, her breasts had also grown from a B-cup to a C, and she cut her ebony curls into a stylish shoulder-length style that would be easier to care for during volleyball season. His dream girl had returned with the body of a voluptuous supermodel, and Aiden knew he would never be the same.

As he stood daydreaming of the lovely Hawaiian woman, a slap on the back brought him back to the present as Marcus resumed his former position leaning against the wall beside him.

Aiden had met the North Carolina native when Marcus had transferred to USC from the University of North Carolina during their junior year. At first, they didn't talk to each other even though they had most of the same classes since they were both engineering majors and both played on the USC basketball team. It wasn't until he had seen the handsome, dark-skinned Marcus talking to Kai after one of their basketball games, did he take notice of the man trying to usurp his territory. That was a strange thought.

Was Kai his territory?

He shook his head pushing the notion from his mind.

Since then, Marcus became another trusted friend and confidant. Not on the same level as Kai, but a real friend, nonetheless. They had even talked about enlisting in the Navy together after college.

"Still haven't grown the stones to ask that female out, huh?" Marcus mused with a thin smile.

"Hey, I got stones," Aiden grunted, obviously agitated. "I've got massive...*stones*."

"Then go ask her to dance." Marcus grabbed him in an inescapable headlock and forced him to focus on Kai.

As he stood hunched over from the position the taller man had him in, he could see Paolo Medici, USC's international student and Polo player from

Rome, making goo-goo eyes at Kai. *His Kai!* The asshole even had the nerve to lead her out onto the crowded dance floor, hand-in-hand, and then pulled her close so not even a sliver of light could be seen between their bodies.

Fuck! Fuck! Fuck!

"What the hell is she doing with that dickhead?" Aiden sputtered as he fought his way out of his friend's death grip. "That guy is a walking STD."

"Looks like they're dancing, dude," Marcus stated casually.

As they stood gaping at Kai and Paolo moving to the rhythm of the upbeat tune, the man's hands inched lower until he had his large caveman digits on Kai's ass.

"What the f—"

"Dear God, savior almighty," Marcus muttered then closed his eyes while making the sign of the cross. "Aiden, you are my boy, but I'm not getting arrested for you on graduation night. I will not come and bail your ass outta jail either. Do you understand me?"

But it was too late. Aiden had already left his buddy and was heading in Kai's direction.

❀

"You are a great dancer," Paolo whispered in her ear as he ground his hips against her pelvis.

"Thanks." Kai tried to push the human octopus away, but he was a solid wall of muscle.

"Come with me back to my apartment?" he glowered, baring his teeth in a feral smile, making her feel uncomfortable.

"I can't. I've got to finish packing," Kai lied hoping to derail his obviously lascivious plans. "You seem like a nice… oh damn… just let me go."

"C'mon, Kay." The thickly accented Italian held her tighter against his chest.

"It's Kai," she huffed, trying to remove his digits from the position they claimed.

Paolo's eyes narrowed with confusion as he asked, "What?"

"My name you idiot." Kai rolled her eyes, annoyance clouding their usual brilliance. "One more thing—" her voice became dangerously low, "—take your hands off of my ass. Right. The. Hell. Now."

"Whatever."

"No dickhead, not *'whatever'*," Aiden sneered. "Get your hands off of her."

"Sure. Okay," Paolo smirked, eyes narrowing. "She's probably a bad lay anyway."

Before Aiden could defend her honor, Kai turned quickly, her right knee suddenly connected to the crude man's crotch. Paolo writhed in agony, but still had the strength to push her away. The unexpected motion caused her to lose balance. Aiden watched helplessly as she fell to the floor and landed on her left wrist. Without another word, Aiden's massive fist made contact with the other man's chin. There was a loud crack, and the sleazy jerk went down for the count.

Trying to subdue his temper, Aiden helped her up, careful not to jostle her hand.

"How's your wrist?"

"Its fine," she fibbed, protectively cradling the injured area.

As gently as possible, he touched her wrist, but she winced and pulled away.

"You are not fine. Let's go."

"Aiden, I said I'm fine," she insisted for the tenth time.

Ignoring her statement, he placed the frozen bag of peas back on her swollen wrist.

"Is this too cold?"

"No," Kai answered with a smile. "Stop being such a worrywart."

Hesitantly, he ran his knuckles down her cheek, stopping momentarily to run a slightly calloused thumb over her sensitive lips. It took all of her self-control to hold back a needy whimper. Dare she admit she was enjoying the feel of his exploring palm against her sensitized skin? The rough texture created a trail of need that started at his touch and snaked down to her abdomen, then further to her groin causing heat to pool in her sex.

It was then she noticed his hand looked as swollen as her wrist. Reluctantly, she stood and walked over to Aiden's freezer in search of another bag of frozen vegetables.

"Give me your hand," she commanded as he sat staring up at her with his mouth slightly ajar. His gaze fixed on her chest; she shrugged it off. It wasn't the first time she'd caught him ogling her breasts. She figured he was a man and that came with the territory.

Quite out of character, he did as he was told, studying her intently as she arranged the frozen produce over his bruised knuckles.

"Ouch! You nymph!" his words came without heat as he smiled up at her.

"Cretan," she mimicked, smiling back. "Thank you."

"What for?"

"For going all white knight on me earlier," she smirked at the memory of Paolo getting clobbered.

"The guy was an asshole," he chuckled. "He deserved it. Plus, you did a great job on your own. I'm sure every time he feels an ache in his balls, he'll think of you."

Laughter bubbled up at the sympathetic groan Aiden made. Turning away, Kai made a move toward the kitchen, but the over-grown Boy Scout she'd just shared a tender moment with pulled her down onto his lap. She couldn't subdue the giggle that escaped.

"Where do you think you are going, Ali'ikai Leilani Kapahu?"

She shuddered even though it wasn't chilly in the least.

"Don't say my name like that," she blushed. "You make it sound so *dirty*."

That made him chuckle.

"If you must know, I am going to the kitchen to put back these bags," she mumbled, her mouth going dry.

"I haven't given you permission to go anywhere," he tried stalling, missing her already.

"Did you just say you didn't give *me* permission?" she gasped playfully.

"Uh-huh," he managed to say without breaking a smile.

"Don't make me go all Kung-Fu on you, Mr. Kaplan."

His chuckle transformed into a loud laugh. The sound sent ripples of desire down her spine.

"Why would you ruin such a beautiful moment?" she scolded without heat.

"It's just the way I roll," he replied with a boyish lilt to his voice.

"What are you, *Don Kaplan*?" Kai gave an unladylike snort.

"Hey, I could be," Aiden reminded. "I'm half Italian."

Kai wiggled again while elbowing him in the ribcage. Finally, he released her with a litany of swears. His heart was hers and she didn't even know it.

For a brief moment, he sat contemplating whether or not to reveal his feelings, but instead he suddenly stood and opened his arms. Without hesitation, and to his relief, Kai walked into his warm embrace. To her, the man smelled amazing, a combination of sandalwood soap, musk, and his own essence. It was heady and it was making her upper lip sweat, and desire filled her once again.

"Aiden?"

"Uh huh," he mumbled; his nose buried deep in her tresses.

"I want you to be my first," the words tumbled out of her mouth in a rushed jumble.

"Your first what?" he questioned, tightening his embrace.

"I want you to take my virginity," she clarified on an exhale.

At her outlandish request, Aiden began to choke on his own spit.

When he finally regained his composure, he managed to sputter, "Pardon me?"

Embarrassment immediately flooded her cheeks.

"I'm going to be twenty-three in a few months, and I'll be going out into the real world," she nervously explained. "I don't know when and if I'll find anyone anytime soon and you're my best friend, the person I trust the most. I would rather give it to you than some random guy."

Aiden pulled away, eyes swirling with confusion.

"What do you mean you're a v-virgin?"

Totally embarrassed, Kai released him, plopping down on the dining chair he had recently vacated, refusing to meet his disbelieving stare.

"It means I haven't... I don't... damn it...you know what I *'haven't'* done."

To her dismay, he still looked completely and utterly dumbfounded.

"But you can't still be a... *you know*." He waved his hands dismissively towards her lower body. "You're gor...passable. I mean...you wouldn't need to put a bag over your head or anything."

"Thanks for calling me a dog you...you...you know what you are!" Words suddenly eluded her.

Swiftly she stood, almost causing the chair to topple over, grabbed her purse from the tabletop and sprinted toward the front door. The strong tug on her good wrist halted her exit.

"Shit! I'm sorry." Aiden reached down to hold her hands, noticing her palms were sweaty, but he didn't care. It only made him hold them tighter. Clearing his throat, he managed to say, "You are beautiful, the most beautiful woman I've ever seen. And you're smart…and funny…and a total ball-buster." Aiden squeezed her hands gently. "But this is a huge step."

"Please Aiden," she begged. "I've never asked for a favor before. If you care about me at all, you'll agree," her voice was almost too low to hear.

"I don't know about this plan, Kai."

As they stood inches away from each other, foreheads pressed together staring into each other's eyes, the corners of Kai's mouth slowly turned upward into a mischievous, almost scary smile.

"If you don't think you can handle the pressure, you can just say so."

The challenge was made, and she knew she had him. Aiden never backed away from a challenge, especially a challenge from her. She knew him too well.

Blue eyes narrowed at her unfounded implication.

"I can handle the pressure," he stated confidently.

"You haven't had a steady girlfriend in a while, you might be rusty," she reminded, batting her long eyelashes.

"Fuck that shit!" he growled. "I'm a love machine."

"Sure. Right," she provoked, knowing she had won. "Whatever you say, Kaplan."

Just as she had hoped, his head lowered, but stopped an inch before their lips touched.

"Kai, it seems kinda weird for us to do…*it*."

She was quiet for a moment, deciding on her next move.

"Don't worry about it," she purred. "I'm going to find Marcus and let him...*do it*."

All the blood drained out of Aiden's face.

"You *wouldn't* dare," his voice was practically a growl.

"But I *would* dare," she hissed back.

When he didn't make any motions to continue, Kai moved toward the door again, but didn't get more than a couple of feet before her body was pulled back. Aiden's strong arms encircled her waist and held her immobile against a muscular torso. The moan caught in her throat when she looked into his eyes and saw a shade of blue she'd never seen before, a deeply hypnotic sapphire.

"Come here, woman."

CHAPTER TWO

Six years later…

"Are you coming out with us tonight, Kai?" The newly divorced labor and delivery nurse asked as they walked through the hallway of the military hospital. "You know Wednesdays are ladies' night at the Buho Cantina."

"No, not tonight," Kai smiled. "I have a special dinner date tonight with my guy."

"That's so sweet," the other woman cooed with jealousy. "Where are you two going?"

"We're staying in," she giggled girlishly. "He's cooking."

"Well, damn!" the middle-aged, coffee-skinned nurse exclaimed. "I was married to Marvin for over twenty-five years and the only thing he ever cooked for me was macaroni and cheese from a box and it wasn't even a name brand. Cheap bastard."

"Yeah, A.J. spoils me," Kai sighed happily.

"I'll rent him from you," her friend beamed with all seriousness.

"Evelyn, you are crazy," Kai chuckled while trying not to blush.

"Yeah, so they keep telling me." The nurse responded, rolling her eyes. "I'm finished with my shift. How 'bout you?"

"I've got one more patient to see then I'm outta here," she informed, checking her chart once more.

"Cool beans," Evelyn grinned. "I'll see you tomorrow?"

"Yup," Kai grinned back. "I'll be here."

"Bye, sweetie."

Evelyn gave her a quick hug.

"See you tomorrow," the overly stressed physical therapist waved.

Needless to say, Kai's thirty-minute physical therapy session with sixty-five-year-old, retired gunnery sergeant, Henry Spencer, went like a breeze. Before long, she was back at the third floor PT desk, signing out for the day. Anxiously, she glanced at the wall clock, 4:25 p.m., just five more minutes and she'd be home free.

A hollow click came from the hospital intercom system, followed by a pleasant female voice.

"We need a physical therapist in emergency exam room three, STAT," the faceless voice announced.

"Kai, could you please take that?" Angela, the PT department's receptionist pleaded. "Tony has already left for the day. His wife's having her first ultrasound today,"

Kai smiled.

"Sure, no worries."

In a rush to make her dinner date, she immediately went down to the emergency room, checked-in at the nurses' station for a briefing, then headed to exam room three. Automatically, she reviewed the patient's chart then pasted on her smile before stepping into the small room to begin her consultation.

Just as she had done countless times before, she pushed open the door, but still hadn't looked up.

"*Aloha*," she greeted pleasantly. "I see your left knee is giving you some trouble today, Mister—"

"Holy shit!" The familiar voice reached into her womb. "Amazon? Is that you?"

In a dazed stupor, she glanced up, her tongue going numb, palms itching and sweating like crazy.

"Aiden?" she whispered then cleared her throat…once…twice.

Oh, God! Please let this be a dream.

"Aiden, what are you doing here?"

Stiffly he rose, closing the distance between them in two long strides, embracing her in a gentle hug while burying his nose in her hair as was his custom.

Breathing suddenly became an issue.

"Aiden, oh, my gracious! What the hell are you doing here?"

On my island.

In my hospital.

In my arms.

"I'm stationed at Pearl-Hickam for the next twelve weeks on a special project," he quickly explained. "I got in a few days ago."

"You joined the Navy?" she gulped loudly. "Like your dad?"

"Yup."

He smelled soooo good!

Focus, Kai!

Focus!

How could it be that the man was *even more* breathtaking? Tall, leanly muscled, goldenly-tanned, except now he had filled-in and no longer looked like a lanky coat hanger, but a rugged *LL Bean* model. Even in his long navy basketball shorts and standard Navy t-shirt, he was devastating. His dark brown hair was shorter now and his face was clean shaven instead of sporting his former sexy five-o'clock stubble that he had in college.

Damn it! He was still fine!

Holding an oncoming panic attack at bay, she tried to push him away, but he refused to release her, only pulling back a few inches. Then she saw them, *really saw them*, those big, beautiful gray-blue eyes. Immediately, her chest tightened.

"Aiden, I need you to sit so I can examine your knee," Kai commanded, trying to calm her breathing.

Obediently, he pulled her toward the paper covered examination table then sat, watching her intently as she touched, bent, and stretched his injured leg, feeling the muscle movement below the skin. It was inflamed and radiating heat, which concerned her.

She frowned.

"This is the knee you hurt in college." It wasn't a question.

She remembered all too well the game between USC and UCLA, the game Aiden scored the winning basket seconds before the final buzzer sounded. It was also the game that a less than sportsmanlike opponent pushed him while doing said game-winning shot, causing him to land badly, tearing his ACL.

He had to have surgery and was out for the rest of the season. Kai also remembered cooking for him, bringing him his class assignments and cleaning his apartment, without any thanks and many of an argument and name-calling. Which he frequently started. Aiden was a terrible patient then, and she was certain he'd be even worse now.

"How did you mess it up this time? Was this another one of your infamous basketball showdowns?" she calmly reprimanded.

He dropped his head in mock shame; she knew him too well.

"I'm going to send you for x-rays, so I can see what's going on with this knee of yours," she explained. "However, you're going to have to take it easy for the next month or so."

Shaking those sable locks he stood again, placing his hands on her shoulders, the gentle touch eliciting emotions she hadn't felt in years. Desire. Hot, sweaty, and downright...*Dirty*, flooded her cerebral cortex.

"Come have a drink with me after we're done with my x-rays," he requested, finally releasing her.

Before he could touch her again, she nervously took a step backward.

"I can't."

"Why not?" he sulked. "We haven't seen each other in…"

"…forever?" Kai finished. "Because I have plans tonight."

Be strong! And whatever you do don't look into those eyes.

Oh, crap when did they get so dark?

Those beautiful orbs of liquid sapphire were shifting, glowing, radiating so much heat Kai had to look away to keep her wits.

"What about tomorrow after your shift?" he persisted.

"I'm not sure, Aiden."

Determined to see her again, he paused for a moment apparently contemplating his next move. Then the college friend she remembered was back and in full pain-in-the-ass form.

As was his habit, he crossed his well-defined arms across an impossibly lick-able chest.

"If you don't agree to have a drink with me, I'll show up here every day and serenade you with disco tunes. Really bad disco tunes, in front of your coworkers in full 70's costume." Then he tilted his head robotically. "And afro wig."

Heaven's no!

"You *wouldn't* dare!" she gasped, putting nothing past him.

"Oh, but I *would* dare," he challenged, experiencing a twinge of fear.

"That's blackmail," she accused with a scowl.

"Blackmail is such an ugly, ugly word, Kai," he mocked in retaliation.

"Yeah," she huffed. "And it's coming from an ugly, *ugly* man."

In an overly dramatic fashion, he grasped his chest in mock horror, threw himself backwards, landing on the table causing the paper to tear, and gave an exaggerated sigh.

"You wound me," the officer sighed. "Cut me to the bone. It would be less painful if you rip out my intestines and use them for jump ropes. I'll never survive the—"

"Imbecile," she accused with a snort.

"Wench," he replied with a wink.

"For heaven's sake."

Kai walked over to where he lay. Looked down into those eyes and placed her hand on his much larger one.

"Okay." She swallowed what little moisture she had left in her mouth. "I'll meet you tomorrow, five o'clock at *Duke's*. Do you know where it is?"

"I'll find it."

Then he sat up like a good little boy and remained quiet for the rest of the examination.

Bang! Bang! Bang!

Startled, Marcus jumped up from his reclined position on his favorite armchair and jogged toward the loud banging on his front door. Swinging it open wide without thinking, his best friend and worst nightmare, Aiden Kaplan, burst into his foyer almost knocking him on his ass.

"What the hell?!" Marcus lowered his voice to a whisper and glanced over his massive shoulder towards the hallway leading to the back of the bungalow. "Vanessa is taking a nap and I'm enjoying the quiet."

The dark-skinned, African-American sailor looked terrified.

"Do you know she had me up at two o'clock in the morning making her peanut butter, ham and banana pepper sandwiches," his voice dropped an octave. "With coffee ice cream sodas."

He shook his head.

"I can't wait until this pregnancy is over."

Aiden patted him on the shoulder.

"Well, at least she stopped throwing up."

Marcus smiled in agreement.

"Marcus?" A delicate, feminine voice drifted down the hall.

"Yes, my love," Marcus grimaced.

"Who are you talking to?"

"Aiden stopped by," the flustered man confessed.

"Really?" her voice softened. "Hi, Aiden!"

Aiden smiled.

"Hey, Vanessa. How are you feeling?"

"I'm well, thanks" the unseen mom-to-be revealed cheerfully. "But I'd feel even better if my husband, who got me into this situation, would make me a sandwich."

Marcus laughed then headed to the kitchen beckoning Aiden to follow.

"I'm on it, babe."

"Marcus?"

"Yes, dear?"

"I love you."

The other man grinned from ear to ear.

"Me too."

Aiden punched him on the back.

"You are such a pansy-ass. Could we get back to me now, please?"

"Ouch!" Marcus rubbed the injured area. "Go ahead."

Excitedly, Aiden paced back and forth like a caged panther completely forgetting about his bad knee.

"I just saw, Kai...*my Kai*, just a few minutes ago. She looks the same, except better...*hotter*. She gained a little more weight and has bigger boobs...eyes...I meant eyes, but she's still gorgeous! And still funny as hell. I missed her, a lot."

"Damn it! Stay still," the future father scolded. "You're making me dizzy."

They sat on the couch after Marcus delivered his wife a peanut butter and salami sandwich and a glass of orange juice. Aiden finally took a deep breath after breaking every traffic law to get to his friend's house with the big news.

"My knee was bothering me after the basketball game this afternoon, right? Right," he paused as Marcus shook his head in agreement. "I went to the Naval Health Clinic; you know the one adjacent to the shipyard on base to get it checked out. I'm sitting there waiting when all of a sudden, the *physical therapist* on duty comes to check me out."

Marcus's eyes narrowed as his jaw fell open, eyes bugging out like a chameleon.

"Kai works on base... this base, and she *checked* you out?"

"Don't say *checked* like that, it makes me itchy."

Aiden dropped his head into his hands as the truth finally sunk into his brain. The seductress of his wet dreams, the temptress of his every waking hour, the vixen who stole his heart nine years ago was back in his life.

"What do I do?"

"Did you set up a time to see her again, outside of work?"

"Of course, I did. I'm not an idiot." Aiden ran his hands through his hair in frustration. "We're meeting for drinks tomorrow at *Duke's* after work."

"Good, the first part of the mission is a go," Marcus encouraged. "Did you ask her if she's married?"

"No," Aiden scowled. "But I didn't see a wedding ring."

Marcus shook his head.

"I don't know. Before Vanessa went on maternity leave, she didn't wear her wedding ring to work either because she didn't want it to get damaged."

Well, shit!

Aiden leaned back against the soft leather material.

"I guess I'll find out tomorrow."

"I'm home!" Kai announced as she entered her parents' home. "Where is everybody?"

Quickly, she took off her white lab coat and shoes and deposited her purse on the foyer table.

Kai had always loved her parents' house located in Hawaii Kai, on the Southeastern side of Oahu. The contemporary, two-story dwelling with cathedral ceilings, gleaming hard-wood floors, fully-equipped kitchen with all the bells and whistles, and an unobstructed view of Koko Crater had always appealed to her. Her parents had even splurged and put in a large, in-ground swimming pool a couple of years ago. One day she hoped to own a home just like it.

"*Aloha*, sweetheart!" her father, Joseph, called from the kitchen.

"*Aloha*. Where's A.J.?" she questioned, almost afraid to hear the answer.

Her father smirked then nodded toward the formal dining room.

"He's been waiting for you in there since five o'clock."

"Oh, no," Kai's voice lowered. "I had a last-minute patient I had to see."

"Are you okay?" Joseph studied her tense expression. "You don't look okay."

Happy to be home, she tiptoed and gave her dad a hug.

"No," she confirmed. "Not really, but I'll tell you all about it later."

"Sure, no worries."

"*Mahalo*," she thanked him in Hawaiian.

Leaving her father in the kitchen, she silently made her way to the dining area, careful not to make any noise. Before she had fully stepped into the room, a short, missile-like object pounced on her, dragging her down to the hardwood floors.

"Mommy, mommy! What took you so long?"

The angelic face that looked up at her never failed to steal her breath just like his father.

Oh, dear, his father!

"I'm sorry, little man." Kai kissed him on each cheek, his forehead and then the tip of his lightly freckled nose. He looked into her eyes, smiling widely, his gray-blue eyes studying her sad expression.

"Bad day at work?" A.J. questioned, reminding her that he was much too perceptive for a five-year-old.

"No, it wasn't a bad day…just an unexpected one." Gently, she combed her fingers through his silky, ebony strands. His complexion was a few shades lighter than her own, but still naturally golden. His cheekbones were highly-chiseled combined with a flirtatious grin that got him noticed by girls of all ages. There was no doubt he was his daddy's boy.

"Oh," was her son's only response.

Before he could escape, Kai picked him up and placed him on a dining chair.

"What did you make us for our special dinner?" she asked, sitting down across from him.

A.J. winked.

"Pappy helped me make grilled cheese sandwiches, hot dogs with mustard, and pineapple lemonade."

Thoughtfully, he started putting food on her plate.

"No dessert?" she teased.

"You didn't let me finish," he smiled good-naturedly.

Holding up her hands in surrender, she apologized.

"Sorry, my love. What's for dessert?"

Then she took a bite of the sandwich.

Enthusiastically, her son bolted from the dining room into the kitchen almost knocking over his grandfather in the process.

"Ay, you're gonna kill me and destroy my house," her father chastised, but his smile could be heard in his deep, rough voice.

"Sorry, Pappy," her baby boy giggled, and it was the best sound she'd heard all day.

"What are you gonna do, Kai?" Leilani sipped at her tea as they sat on the lanai enjoying the warm, hibiscus-scented breeze. The evening sky was clear with a thousand twinkling stars staring down, all eavesdropping on their tense conversation.

"I have to tell him," she sighed, taking a large gulp of her own tea, which was now revoltingly cold. "It's obvious his idiot of a father never gave him my message that I was pregnant all those years ago. I know I have to tell him."

"Why didn't you contact Aiden directly when you found out you were expecting?" Joseph asked, his attention temporarily distracted from his newspaper.

Saddened at the memory, Kai sat back on the floral patio chair cushion.

"I did," she admitted meekly. "I left messages on his cell. I wrote letters and mailed them to his father's home address, but they all came back unopened. Finally, I contacted his dad at his office in Annapolis and asked if he would break the news to Aiden. I expected Aiden would get in touch with me, but he never did. I assumed he didn't give a damn."

"Hmm," her mother hummed, staring straight ahead.

"Why are you humming?" Kai sat straighter.

"It will all work out," Leilani comforted with a chuckle. "That young man has always loved you,"

"You're so off base," Kai snorted, running a nervous finger around the lip of the cup.

"I'm no fool," her mother's eyes narrowed. "Aiden would look at you like you were a prime rib buffet with all the fixings."

A loud snort escaped Joseph's chest.

"Do you think we didn't notice how much the two of you argued? Or the heated glances you shared? There was such longing between the both of you it's a miracle you didn't spontaneously combust." Joseph chuckled. "Don't even get me started on the hitting."

"I didn't hit him that much," she protested, feeling her cheeks redden.

Joseph laughed.

"Any reason to touch him," he accused playfully. "And what about the practical jokes you played on each other?"

Kai frowned.

"Ah! Ha! Exactly!"

She jumped out of her seat and paced the smooth wooden deck.

"Heat isn't everything. We argued all the time. He played practical jokes on me until I had no choice but to retaliate. Did I ever tell you about the time he filled my volleyball sneakers with shaving cream? It was before the championship game too. What kind of person does that?"

She sat again.

"I'll tell you what kind of person does that. Not one that loves you!" she sputtered indignantly. "That's for damn sure!"

Joseph Kapahu raised his hand as if he were back in school trying to get the teacher's attention.

"Before I asked your mother on our first date," he cleared his throat. "I wrote my name on her car with a Sharpie."

Leilani's head snapped up, pinning her husband with an icy glare.

"It was you who did that?" his wife hissed.

"Yup," Joseph grinned.

"I thought that was Danny Wu." She looked mortified. "I beat the boy within an inch of his life, then I told his parents, and they grounded him for that whole summer."

"Yup," her husband grinned wider.

"Joseph, why didn't you say something?"

His wife was about to disembowel him.

The gentle giant simply chuckled again.

"I wanted him to know you were mine."

"We weren't even dating then," Leilani groaned.

"It didn't matter," Joseph kissed her cheek sweetly. "You were mine from the day you ran over my foot with your shopping cart."

CHAPTER THREE

Aiden left his temporary office on the Navy base two hours early to get a haircut and a shave. Wanting to look his best, he bought a new pair of jeans and dress shirt at his favorite department store, and got his rental car cleaned just in case he could talk Kai into going back to his apartment. He even got to *Duke's* on Waikiki Beach thirty minutes early to snag a table with the best view of the ocean. Everything had to be perfect…for her.

He sat nervously the whole time, glancing from his watch to the bar's entrance every few minutes. The waiting was agony, but at 4:55 p.m. movement near the front door caught his attention. It was Kai.

Finally.

Of course, she looked incredible sporting dark, form-fitting jeans that hugged all of those tantalizing curves, a white sheer peasant top with a scoop neckline, strappy white sandals showing off her well-manicured toes and her ebony curls cascading a few inches past her shoulders. Just like he'd remembered, the only make-up she wore was eyeliner and nude lip gloss. Aiden made a quick pass with his hand over his mouth making sure there was no drool.

As usual, Kai had the attention of almost every man at the bar and even a few of the women. Her naturally curly hair fluttered sensuously as the ocean-kissed breeze ran invisible fingers through the silky strands. Aiden rubbed his hand over his heart trying to ease the dull ache there.

Automatically, he stood, walking towards her like a man on a mission. Stopping about a foot away from her, he leaned down and took her right hand in his. When those amber irises met his, the world around them ceased to exist and for one brief moment he was terrified.

"Aloha," she greeted shyly.

When his mind cleared, he noticed Kai's palm was sweaty. Relief washed over him to know she was just as affected as he was.

"Witch," he grinned, raking her body from head to toe then back again, his gaze resting on her chest.

"Still a pervert, I see," Kai chuckled, becoming more at ease.

"You look great, *really, really* great!"

He winked when she rewarded him with a blush.

Hugging her briefly, he inhaled the whimsical jasmine fragrance surrounding her before leading her to their table, still holding her hand. Chivalrously, he pulled out her chair and waited as she sat. Then he sat on the adjacent chair, pulling it close enough for their thighs to touch. They ordered drinks and a Pupu platter, making small talk while waiting for their server to return with their items.

"You're an electrical engineer and a lieutenant in the Navy," Kai restated with a grin that stole his senses. "Good for you."

Playfully, she slapped him on the arm.

"I always knew you'd make something of yourself."

That made him blush.

"Should I salute you?"

Their eyes met and Aiden felt a familiar tingling in the pit of his stomach.

"Only if you want to," he replied with a chuckle.

Although, truth be told, part of him was already *saluting* her. He'd keep that information to himself.

"I joined the Navy fresh out of USC, finished some graduate courses at Annapolis the year after enlisting," he added. "I know you're a physical therapist but tell me about the rest of your life."

Aiden paused as Ken their waiter delivered their drinks: a lava flow for her, which was a pina colada with fresh pureed strawberries and a Corona with lime for himself. As soon as Ken scurried away, he asked the question that had been burning his tongue since yesterday.

"Are you married?" he asked, clearing his throat.

His question almost made her choke on her tropical libation. When she regained her equanimity, she whispered her answer.

"No. I'm not married."

A slow smile spread across her features as Aiden released a breath, he didn't know he was holding. It felt like the weight of the world lifted off of his shoulders.

"Good," he beamed. "What about a boyfriend?"

Kai shook her head.

"Whew! Terrific! Hold on one minute, please."

Grabbing his cell phone from his back pocket, he sent a text message. Kai's eyebrow arched making him blush.

"I'm answering a text from Marcus."

Uncharacteristically, her forehead wrinkled in thought.

"You guys still keep in touch?"

"Marcus and I joined the Navy together, even attended Annapolis together," he confided, nodding in the affirmative.

"What's he up to?" she asked, curious about the man she regarded as a lifelong friend.

"He's married," Aiden smirked.

Amber eyes opened wide.

"Are you serious?"

"Yeah." He rubbed the back of his nape. "He and Vanessa are expecting their first child in a few months. They're on the island as well, living in temporary family housing on base while we work on the project at Pearl-Hickam."

"Wow!" she declared, but her eyes were cloudy with some unknown emotion.

"I can't believe it sometimes myself," the naval officer admitted sheepishly.

Without warning, Kai's expression hardened.

"It's great you two are still such good friends."

Her emotionless tone disturbed him more than he cared to admit.

"Why the long face?" he queried.

Aiden pushed a stray curl away from her exotic, almond-shaped eyes.

She hesitated for only a second or two.

"Why didn't you contact me after graduation, Aiden?" Her hands were grasped tightly on her lap. "Especially after we…"

"…had sex." Aiden noticed her body stiffened.

Her narrowed stare made him shift nervously.

"Correct, after we had *sex*."

After a couple of tense minutes, he finally spoke.

"There's no excuse. None whatsoever, I was young and stupid—"

"You've got that right," she agreed, rolling her eyes. "Did your father tell you I had contacted him trying to locate you?"

"No," Aiden frowned.

"Oh," her voice immediately softened.

Needing to touch her, he reached over, took her hands out of her lap, and placed them on the table with his own covering them.

"You were...correction...you are my best friend." Aiden's eyes appeared glassy, the irises a gorgeous sapphire hue. "Would it help my cause to tell you I've thought about you every damn day since then?"

"Maybe," she smirked. The sound making his member harden more than it already was, he shifted trying to get more comfortable.

"I'm sorry, Kai," he sincerely apologized. "I truly am."

A long pregnant moment passed before she spoke again.

"Why aren't you married with little tadpoles of your own, Aiden Joseph Kaplan?"

"I don't know," he mumbled, nervously playing with his napkin. "I didn't date a lot after college."

"No! Way!" Kai's stunned statement made him guffaw.

"It's true," he continued. "I had a girlfriend, Beth, two years ago, but it didn't work out."

"I guess I can't call you a *kolohe* anymore," she sighed.

"And what about you, Ali'ikai Leilani Kapahu?" He loved saying her full name. "Why are you not married? I'm surprised someone hasn't claimed you yet."

"How can you make my name sound so *dirty*?" she blushed, glaring at her long-lost love.

"It's a gift." Aiden's eyes twinkled with amusement.

"Caveman," her voice lowered an octave. "I haven't found the right guy yet."

"Good," he winked, feeling more comfortable.

The rest of the evening went by quickly as they spoke about their jobs, their common lack of a social life and past college shenanigans. Aiden hadn't felt this happy since their last night together in Los Angeles.

Beth, his ex-girlfriend, wanted a commitment, but he couldn't bring himself to do it. After only six months of dating, he broke up with her, knowing it wouldn't be fair to lead her on. Since then, dating seemed more like a chore. Instead, he buried himself in his work, climbing the military career ladder and living vicariously through Marcus.

His buddy, also an engineer, had joined the Navy with Aiden, but that was where their lives diverted. Unlike Aiden, who was married to his job, Marcus met and married Vanessa within the first month they enlisted. Vanessa was the nurse who gave them physicals before starting boot camp. Marcus practically proposed on their third date. Four years later they were expecting their first child, and for the first time, Aiden felt a twinge of jealousy.

Before he realized it, another two hours had passed as the two old friends chewed the fat, enjoying each other's company. During Kai's story of a patient who kept stripping off his clothes during therapy sessions, her cell phone began to vibrate.

"Excuse me for a minute," she apologized. "I have to get this."

"Of course," he replied, admiring her as she stood.

Stepping to the far end of the outside patio area, she answered the call. Aiden's heart began beating faster the longer he stared at her. When she returned, a disappointed look shadowed her lovely features.

"I'm sorry, Aiden, but I have to leave."

"Why?" he almost pouted like a toddler, voice sounding desperate even to his ears. "Is something wrong?"

"It's a small family emergency," she replied, gathering up her purse. "Nothing to worry about."

"I'll walk you out. I have an early meeting in the morning."

Promptly, he waved over the waiter, and paid the check. As they leisurely strolled enjoying the temperate March evening, Kai retrieved her car keys from the rather large handbag she carried.

"I had fun tonight," she smiled. "Thank you."

"No thanks necessary," he beamed. "When can I see you again?"

Then she smiled one of those smiles that made him numb from the neck down.

"When do you want to see me?"

"Tomorrow night," he blurted.

It wasn't a request, and at this point, he didn't care if he sounded pathetic or not.

"Tomorrow night sounds good," she agreed, blushing. "Where should we meet? I know a great Japanese steakhouse nearby."

"Come to dinner, my place," he invited. "I'll cook for you."

"You can cook? Since when?" she teased, unsuccessfully hiding her amusement.

"There's more to me than meets the eye," he winked, and swore he heard her breath hitch.

When she spoke next her voice was raspier.

"I see, *Optimus Prime*."

Without being asked, Aiden took her out-held phone and programmed his cell phone number, home address, and office number into the small device.

"Be at my apartment at six."

"That's too early," she informed, reviewing her work schedule in her rapidly racing mind. "What about seven?"

"Seven it is," he beamed, trying to slow his heartbeat.

Lingering for a few more moments, they laughed and flirted, enjoying the comfortable banter before deciding it was time to go. Kai had to go home, and he needed to get his notes together for his meeting in the morning.

The night breeze wafted around them as they left the bar, the unique scent of palm fronds and grilling food tantalizing their senses. High above, the Hawaiian sky was heavy laden with stars, like someone had doused a black canvas with specks of white paint. Leisurely, Aiden walked her to her SUV. It was romantic and a wholly dreamy moment just waiting to be seized.

Every molecule in his body wanted to kiss her, yet he refrained. In the back of his mind, he knew if he kissed her now there would be no way he'd want her to go. He'd take her right there in the middle of the parking lot against her vehicle. Aiden wanted to be inside her again more than he wanted to breathe his next breath, but it would be in the heat of passion. When next they made love, it would be tender and sweet and in his bed.

Unrushed, Kai unlocked the car door, but remained standing beside it leaning her upper body against the frame.

"You better not give me food poisoning tomorrow, Lieutenant Kaplan," she warned, punching him lightly on the arm.

"Devil," Aiden hissed playfully, removing an eyelash from her slightly flushed cheek. Any reason to touch her was good as far as he was concerned.

"Sure," she snorted, her tone dripped sarcasm. "I'm the devil."

"You're going to hurt my feelings, Miss Kapahu."

"We wouldn't want that now, would we?"

"No, we would not."

Unable to resist any longer, Aiden gathered up her silken locks sweeping them aside then pressed his lips against her collarbone.

"*Mmm*, you smell incredible. I bet you taste even better." His hardening cock strained against the rough denim. To his relief, Kai arched her neck to give him better access.

"Aiden?" Her voice sounded more like a contented purr when she spoke and he smiled to himself at the thought he could undo her resistance with one strategically-placed kiss.

"Hmm?" he hummed against her neck.

"What are you doing?"

"What do you think I'm doing?"

"You're starting something that can't be finished in this parking lot," she lightheartedly scolded.

"Sorry. I got carried away," his laugh was low and barely recognizable as he confessed.

"Aiden?"

"Yes, love?"

Love! Damn! Where did that come from?

"Kiss me," she commanded.

"No."

"Why?" she huffed as her body stiffened.

He planted chaste kisses along her throat.

"If I kiss you now, I'm going to want to fuck you. Right. Here. In. This. Parking. Lot." Wickedly punctuating every word with shallow thrusts of his hips knowing she could feel his erection. "Tomorrow. I'll kiss you tomorrow."

"I want you to kiss me...*now*," she demanded, encircling her arms around his neck to secure him in place.

He couldn't subdue the maniacal chuckle that escaped him.

"Tomorrow, my little Hawaiian blossom, have patience."

Those words must not have settled well with Kai, because before he could step back, she yanked his head down and claimed his mouth. He tried not to kiss her back. The Lord help him, he really did try, but Kai's stubbornness wouldn't relent, even though at first, he kept his lips tightly sealed.

"Kiss me, you obnoxious fiend of a man!" she hissed, seductively tugging gently on his lower lip.

Without further pretense, he gave in to her command knowing full well it was futile to resist. Kai was like a dog with a bone, you either gave her what she wanted willingly or prepared to be bitten.

Finally, he did as he was told. His arms came around her slender waist, mouth moving hungrily over hers. While his tongue swept across her lips, urging her to allow him greater access. She tasted like Pina Colada and sinful things and his foundation throbbed in response. Her mouth parted in silent reply, and he took the invitation to slip past her sensuous, full lips. Their tongues sought each other out, dancing against each other in a passionate tango, finding responsive nerve endings and stroking them with velvety licks. She moaned softly before pulling away, ending the most devastating kiss he'd ever had the pleasure of experiencing.

"What's wrong?" Aiden arched a disbelieving brow, his entire body stiffened with fierce desire.

"I really have to go," her voice was raspy, like she'd just woken up. It was sexy as hell.

"One more minute," he pleaded. Sucking her earlobe into his mouth, he played with it with the tip of his tongue. Kai wiggled, trying unsuccessfully to escape his grip. She stopped when she felt the evidence of his arousal against her abdomen. Her almond eyes widened like saucers.

"Aiden," she whispered, trying to get his attention.

"This is what you do to me." He took her hand and placed it over his groin. The heat of her hand through the denim was almost too much to bear. "Ever since you dropped that freaking physics book on me, I've been at a constant half-mast."

A soft moan escaped her when he began to grind his cock into her palm, making him grow until it felt as if the zipper of his jeans would burst.

"I love it when you use sailing terms," Kai giggled.

"Well then, would you care to shiver my timber?"

"Pig!" she chastised, squeezing his swollen member until he pulled away laughing. Quickly climbing into her SUV, she fastened her seat belt, started the engine then looked up at him, eyes shimmering like she was on the verge of crying.

Gently, Aiden closed her door.

"I'll see you tomorrow night, seven o'clock."

She shook her head causing her curls to catch the light of the overhead fluorescent streetlamps.

"Don't be late."

"Aye-aye, Sir," she gave him a mock salute.

Refusing to leave before she was out of sight, Aiden stood staring at Kai's white *Highlander* as it pulled out of the parking lot and up busy Kalakaua Avenue. His heart still pounded in his ears, his erection so painful he couldn't walk.

Damn! Damn! Damn!

He was in so much trouble.

❀

The forty-minute drive back home was one of the most difficult things she'd done in her life. Every instinct she had screamed to turn the car around and claim her man. *Her man.* Instead, she headed to her parents' house in Hawaii Kai.

It didn't help that Aiden looked like he'd just stepped off a Parisian runway, with his black button-down dress shirt rolled to the elbows, loose-fitting dark jeans and black boots. His scent was that all too familiar fragrance of sandalwood, musk, and sexy male. Her panties were soaked from the moment she saw him walking toward her on the deck of the local watering hole.

Surprisingly, her lustful thoughts were manageable during drinks. She'd fooled herself into believing she was out of temptation's way until he looked down at her as they leaned against her *Highlander*, eyes that seductive, dark sapphire.

Damn! The man could kiss.

Her lips still tingled from his touch. Six years was way too long to go without having sex, especially having sex with him.

"How's he feeling?" Kai crossed the room to her son's bed. A.J. was nestled under his *Spiderman* sheets, only a thatch of black hair sticking out.

"His fever broke about an hour ago," Leilani whispered. "I didn't want to disturb your date, but *he* insisted I call."

"I would have been home sooner if you had called." Her features softened as she watched her son sleeping soundly.

"There was no need for you to come home," Leilani grinned. "I've been a mom for over thirty years, raised two healthy children. Fevers don't scare me. How was your date with Aiden?"

"It was amazing," Kai sighed, the sound full of joy. "He's amazing. I'm seeing him tomorrow night. I'm going to ask Koa to watch A.J. for the weekend if that's alright with you?"

"Of course, Kai, your brother will love that," her mother smiled again. "You've been responsible for a very long time. Have some fun. Don't be such an old fuddy-duddy."

"I'll try not to be you," Kai teased.

"Did you tell Aiden about A.J.?"

"Not yet," she whispered.

"Stop putting it off," Leilani lectured. "It'll be worse when you finally tell him. The man has a right to know he has a son, a handsome, intelligent, rascal of a son."

"Yes, I know," Kai frowned.

Smoothing her daughter's hair away from her face, Leilani reminded, "It's going to be fine."

"Thank you, Mama," she said, giving her mother's hand a grateful squeeze.

"Hey."

"Yeah?"

"Are you going to be out overnight?" she probed cautiously.

"I don't know," Kai blushed. "Probably."

Her mother kissed her forehead before heading to bed.

"Aloha au ia 'oe, Kai."

"I love you too."

Leilani left the room and Kai cuddled up next to the sleeping, younger version of the man she loved. He looked so much like his father it made her heart ache. Tenderly, she ran her fingers over his forehead making sure he was still cool. A.J. stirred but didn't wake.

"I have to tell Aiden he has a son."

And she had to do it soon.

CHAPTER FOUR

It was the longest day of her life. After work she raced home, helped A.J. with his homework, got him bathed, dressed and ready for her brother, Koa.

"Where are you going, Mommy?" A.J. questioned as she finished packing his *Iron Man* duffle bag with all of his necessities for spending a carefree weekend with his uncle.

"Umm," she chose her words carefully. "I'm going on a date."

A.J.'s brow rose.

Oh, my goodness!

He was showing more and more of his father's traits with each passing day.

"A date?" he repeated. "Like what people do in the movies?"

"Yes," she grinned. "I guess so."

His brow wrinkled with confusion.

"But you don't go on dates."

"Not usually, but this is an old friend who I haven't seen in a long time," she explained.

"Oh," he responded, watching her with an intense glare. "Do I know him?"

"No, not yet," she explained, smiling down at his perfect little face. "But you will meet him soon. I promise."

The little boy seemed to be considering her words.

"In the meanwhile, Uncle Koa is going to pick you up and you guys are going to spend the whole weekend together."

"Cool!" Her son did a shaka making her grin. "May we go surfing, Mommy?"

"You may," she warily gave permission. "But only if you wear your life jacket."

His face fell.

"Dudes don't wear life jackets to surf," he frowned. "I'll get laughed at."

"Well, *this* dude is going to wear his life jacket if he wants to surf," his mother insisted.

"That's so lame," he mumbled, his brow furrowing with disappointment.

"Aiden Joseph Kapahu," Kai's voice lowered into the 'voice of doom' she'd perfected during her son's short lifespan. "Do not talk back to me."

"Yes, ma'am," the five-year-old sulked.

As they stood in tense silence, a deep, baritone voice coming from the doorway temporarily halted their argument.

"Where's my favorite nephew?"

A.J. ran squealing into his Uncle Koa's arms.

"I'm here, Uncle Koa and I'm ready!"

"Hey, *braddah*!" Koa spun her son around like a human plane. "Are you ready to go catch some waves?"

"Yeah!"

"Solid." Her brother set A.J. down again.

Affectionately, he mussed the little boy's hair as he leaned over to kiss his younger sister's forehead. Even though they were only two years apart and from the same parents, they looked nothing alike. Koa loomed over her at a whopping 6'7" like their father, and unlike Kai, he had straight hair instead of curly, a perfect aquiline nose, hazel eyes and much darker complexion. A surfer at heart, her brother spent every waking hour, *not* on SEAL training or missions, "hanging-ten" on the North Shore.

"Mahalo for keeping A.J. for me."

"No worries," Koa looked at A.J. curiously. "Hey, *brah*, go put your suitcase in the car, okay?"

"Okay," A.J. smiled broadly.

Koa waited for him to leave the room before speaking.

"You're going out with the *haole* tonight," her older brother teased, already knowing the answer.

"Yeah," Kai blushed, avoiding her sibling's lascivious stare.

"Why are you blushing?" Koa continued to poke. "You already made a baby with the guy."

"A baby he doesn't know about," his sister frowned.

The strapping officer looked at her with a sympathetic expression.

"When are you going to tell him?"

"This weekend," she answered, biting her bottom lip nervously.

Koa smiled right before he jumped on A.J.'s bed, grabbed a pillow, and began hugging and kissing it.

"Oh, Aiden. Love of my life…father of my child. I want you. Take me. Take me…you big, strong, sailor."

"He's an engineer, a lieutenant actually," she laughed at her brother's overly dramatic faux love scene.

"If he's in the Navy, he's a sailor," Koa educated. "Doesn't matter if he's a grunt or an officer."

She pulled the pillow out of his arms and hit him hard across the face.

"Nervous?" he asked.

"A little bit." Kai bit her lip again, trying to calm her nerves. "He's going to hate me."

Protectively, Koa pulled her down onto his lap and held her.

"He might be a little angry…maybe a lot angry—"

"Great!" she exclaimed with exasperation. "Thanks a lot."

"But he'll get over it, *eventually*," Koa tried to comfort.

"I'm so glad you decided *not* to be a grief counselor," she jibbed sarcastically.

"Once he meets A.J., he's going to fall in love with him, okay?" he reiterated, rolling his eyes,

"Okay," she mumbled below her breath, still not convinced that everything would be alright.

Just as she was about to ask him a question, her son. came barreling into the room, jumping on his uncle's chest with the force of a freight train.

"Let's go! Let's go!"

"Ok, ok," Koa picked him up and put him in a fireman's hold. "Let's go catch some waves!"

"Mommy says I have to wear my life jacket," A.J. informed from his upside-down position over his uncle's broad shoulder.

"Really?" Koa rolled his eyes. "That's so lame."

A.J. shook his head in agreement.

"That's what I told her."

Kai could only roll her eyes at the both of them.

Aiden couldn't help staring at the woman standing nervously in his doorway.

"You look beautiful."

"So do you," Kai blushed.

Playfully, Aiden's brow rose.

"Guys aren't beautiful, but thank you for the compliment," he stated matter-of-factly then winked to soften his statement. "Come in. I hope you're hungry. Dinner is almost ready."

"It smells great in here," she complimented, stepping over the threshold of his temporary housing.

"I should hope so," he grumbled, unable to take his eyes off of her. "I've been cooking practically all afternoon."

It was less than twenty-four hours since he'd last seen her, but it seemed like an eternity. Aiden watched as she entered his small apartment and stood in the middle of the living room, hands clasped together so tightly her knuckles were turning white. She reminded him of the girl he had met nine years ago, shy and out of her element.

Automatically, he scanned her from head to toe. Kai looked casual but breathtaking. Wearing white shorts that hit her mid-thigh making her toned legs appear even longer than they already were, a pale blue ribbed tank top that clung to her breasts like a second skin and plain white Nike sneakers. Her hair was in a neat bun with a few curly tendrils framing her face. Unlike the previous evening, she wore no make-up at all and although she was in her natural state, she was still the most exquisite creature he'd ever seen.

"You're staring," Kai smiled.

"Yes, I am," he smiled back.

"Why?"

"Because I can't believe you're here with me after all these years," he answered with all sincerity.

"Flatterer," she blushed. The glimmer in her amber eyes devastated him.

Silently, he glided to where she stood like a deer in the sights of a wolf. He liked that she was nervous. It made him feel powerful, captivating...

dangerous. All the things he didn't feel at the moment, but he didn't want her to know that.

Like the predator he *wasn't*, Aiden stalked her until he stood mere inches in front of her. His chest almost bumping her adorable pert nose, without preamble he tugged her into a hug. Time stood still as they held each other. Slender hands stroked his back causing his muscles to tense against their long steady glide.

Lifting her chin slightly, he leaned down securing his lips over hers. His tongue parted her mouth and dipped inside for a quick swipe before sliding free in a slow, wet withdrawal. Unable to speak, they stood panting, catching their breath and regaining valuable brain function, their bodies still pressed securely together.

"Let's eat," Aiden requested, taking her hand in his and led her to the breakfast bar.

Kai seemed surprised to find the bar set with matching plates, wine glasses, and real silverware. Aiden chuckled to himself, remembering their college days when his cupboards held nothing but disposable plates, two hand-me-down plastic tumblers and an array of convenience store eating utensils. She looked impressed.

"Would you like some wine?" he offered, wanting to impress her even more with his newly attained culinary prowess. "I hope you like merlot?"

"Merlot would be lovely," she replied, looking up at him coyly, batting those long, thick, dark lashes.

Dinner was delicious if he said so himself. He'd made meatloaf, mashed potatoes, and sautéed green beans. He'd bought a fruit tart from a local French bakery for dessert knowing she loved fresh fruit, but that he would save for later.

They spent most of the time in comfortable silence, reminding him of their long time friendship. She made him feel relaxed, more relaxed than he'd felt since their time at university. Once more, he felt that ache in his chest and swiftly began clearing away the now empty plates.

A sound similar to a purr escaped her lips.

"That was scrumptious," she complimented the chef. "Where did you learn to cook?"

"Promise not to laugh," he implored.

"I make no such promise," Kai replied dryly, holding back a snicker.

Aiden hesitated briefly.

"I'm hooked on the *Food Network*," he admitted.

From out of nowhere, a loud peal of laughter reached his ears.

"You promised not to laugh!"

"I made no such promise."

Kai laughed so hard she almost fell off the backless, leather barstool.

"That's the last time I ever share something so personal with you," he declared with mock indignation.

"I'm sorry," she gasped breathlessly. "I really am."

Placing her hand over her mouth, she tried to contain the eruption of giggles attempting to escape.

"No, you're not!" he chuckled too.

"No, I'm really not!" she roared once again, this time miscalculating her precarious position on the edge of the barstool and almost fell off.

In the blink of an eye, Aiden was standing in front of her.

"Succubus."

"Satyr," she snorted.

Aiden's brow winged.

"Satyr? I'll show you who's a satyr."

"Animal," she taunted good-naturedly.

Both brows rose this time.

"I'm an animal? Me?" he leered. "That's it. You shall be punished for your lack of respect you cold-hearted nymph."

Aiden wiggled his long digits. It took a second or two for Kai's brain to register what was coming next, even then she could only gawk in shock. Instead, she stayed put.

"Aiden," she warned. "Don't you dare tickle me!"

"Oh," he scoffed. "I'm going to tickle you and enjoy doing it."

"If you do I'll hot wax your eyebrows off while you sleep," her voice was low and menacing and a tad bit scary.

"You wouldn't dare!" Aiden knew, without a doubt, Kai would follow through with the threat. She was evil like that.

"Oh, but I would dare," she promised with a mischievous grin.

With those five little words, the gauntlet had been thrown down and the game was afoot.

Before she could convince him otherwise, his hands were on her, finding the tickle-sensitive spots and torturing her unmercifully. He got in a few tickles, according to the loud squeals echoing through his apartment. He hoped none of his neighbors heard and called the cops. That's all he would need, but hearing Kai's eardrum bursting cries he was willing to make the sacrifice.

"Aiden, stop it! Right! Now!" she panted.

"Say the magic word!" he ordered, enjoying the upper hand.

"Asshole!" she growled like a lioness.

"No, no, no," he grinned. "That's not the magic word."

"Please…oh goodness…please," she begged.

"Still not the word I was looking for," he informed.

"What's the word? I'll say it!"

"Master," he announced louder than intended.

"Go to hell!" she shouted as the squeals of torture rose in volume.

"No, no, no…go to hell…*master*," he clarified with a smirk.

That word must not have sat well with Kai because before he could get another tickle in, he was kicked in the abdomen by an eight and half, woman's Nike sneaker...hard. The unexpected force caused him to fall backwards onto the carpeted floor while his pain-in-the-ass woman, *no, not his woman, not yet,* jumped off the barstool and ran toward the living room. He stood when he got his wind back and raced in her direction.

"Now, you're really going to get it, Kai," he warned, roguishly.

"Try it and I'll drop kick you," she threatened. "Again."

"I let you do that," he said, trying to save face.

Sarcastically she added, "Of course, you did."

With a cat-like pounce, he sprang forward barely missing the coffee table, but Kai dodged and started heading back to the kitchen. Cutting across the side hallway, he grabbed her around the waist, hauled her against him and strode toward the couch.

"Now, I'm going to spank you," he informed with a smirk.

Her body immediately stilled.

"What?" she snapped; eyes wide.

"You heard me."

Then her face lost all humor.

"Aiden don't do it!" she commanded. "I'll scream. I swear it."

He hitched his eyebrows suggestively.

"Go ahead scream," he smiled. "I happen to like making you scream."

On instinct, Kai's elbow came down with a mighty blow to his solar plexus... hard. The action followed quickly by a kick to his leg and that was it. Aiden went down like a pile of bricks.

A pained groan left him followed by a litany of swears.

*"Ouch! Motherfuc…*I think you broke my knee!"

Kai suddenly halted, looking down at him writhing on the floor grasping his knee. His bad knee. *Crap!* What had she done?

"Aiden?" Tears started to well. "I'm so sorry. I was aiming for your shin. Oh, hell! I didn't mean to… Damn it! Let me take a look."

Submissively, Aiden laid back on the carpet. Eyes closed, breathing heavily. His right hand still gripping the hurt knee.

Switching to work-mode, Kai studied the area, making sure to feel for heat. Bending it gently trying to assess the damage she had caused, guilt threatening to swallow her whole.

"I don't feel any heat, but I'll get you some ice—"

"Oww," he continued to groan and then suddenly stopped.

When Kai glanced up, she saw the smirk on Aiden's face. Immediately, she started moving away, but he was much too fast and far too strong. Without warning, she found herself pinned to the living room carpet with a very sexy, very aroused male on top of her.

"I thought you were hurt?" Amber eyes narrowed suspiciously, but she was grinning.

Before she could protest, he kissed the tip of her nose.

"You did kick my shin and it did hurt," he chuckled moving closer. "But my knee is fine."

"Bastard," she condemned without heat, happy he was not injured, but annoyed for falling for his charade.

Aiden's breathing was erratic and breathy, eyes the shade of blue that thrilled and scared her at the same time.

Calmness spread through her limbs and for an instant, Kai didn't blink. Her gaze held hostage by the way he licked his plump bottom lip. Those strong, well-used hands came up to cup her face. The thumb of his right hand strumming over her mouth in an exploratory touch that caused her to finally exhale the breath she hadn't known she was holding.

"Kiss me," she commanded, her voice sounding shaky. And he did.

Six years' worth of sadness, loneliness, and longing broke through her emotional wall, crumbling the invisible structure into rubble as Aiden's lips brushed against hers. His kisses were gentle at first, barely grazing the sensitive mounds. Expertly, he slipped his tongue inside the cavern of her mouth and stroked it against her own; the taste of merlot, spices, and his unique flavor intermingled between them. Slowly, his tongue slithered around hers, mingling and mimicking the movement of their hips.

Abruptly pulling back, he released a harsh breath.

"Too many clothes," he growled while pulling her tank top up and off, then fumbling at the button of her shorts.

Undoing it herself, she raised her lower body so Aiden could pull them down. In one fell swoop, he had her shorts and panties off and thrown onto the black leather couch less than a foot away.

"Should we go on the couch?" Kai panted breathlessly.

He shook his head, reached behind her, and unhooked her bra. Before he discarded the white lacy undergarment, he examined the tag. One thick, dark brow arched up.

"D-cups?" he whispered.

"Uh huh."

"You've made me an extremely happy man," he praised, licking his lips.

Rolling her eyes, she pulled him down for another kiss. One large hand reached behind him grabbing the back of his dark blue, fitted t-shirt, temporarily removing his lips from hers in order to pull the damn thing off. It landed somewhere near the front door, but he didn't seem to care.

"Help me, Kai," his voice low and husky, almost animalistic, as he placed her hand on the waistband of his shorts.

Following his request, she unbuttoned his khaki cargo shorts and slowly lowered the zipper, the sound almost too loud in the unnaturally quiet room. Instinctively, he raised his hips so she could push both his shorts and boxer briefs all the way down his highly-defined legs. Impatiently, Aiden pulled them completely off, kicking them away from his now naked form.

Anxiously, Kai lay beneath him, eyes closed, afraid to move for fear of it being a figment of her extremely vivid imagination. Many nights she had lain in bed fantasizing about this moment, and now, it was finally here.

"What's wrong?" he whispered, that dark sapphire gaze seeing past her barriers and into her heart…into her soul then tenderly stroked her lips with the slightly calloused pad of his thumb, the movement causing an unsettling rush of liquid warmth to trickle from her core.

"It's nothing," her hands began to visibly shake.

"We can stop," he smiled sincerely. "It will probably kill me, but we don't have to do anything else."

He kissed the tip of her nose again.

"We can watch a movie on *Pay-Per-View* and just hangout. I don't care what we do as long as we're together."

Those words, spoken with such tenderness, were her undoing.

"Be gentle, *kolohe*," she grinned.

"I love it when you call me a rascal," his words broke the tension.

A smile spread across his face before claiming her lips again. It was a slow ravishment of mouths…and lips…and tongues, gliding sinuously over one another. Aiden broke the kiss first, lowering his head to nip, lick, and kiss a trail down her neck.

"I've dreamt of this moment," she whispered to no one in general.

"So have I," he mumbled against her overheated skin.

Curiously, she reached between them, tracing a line with her hand from his pecs, around each flat nipple, down to his well-defined six-pack and into the trail of dark hair leading to his manhood below. When she finally reached her destination, they both moaned.

"This should come with a warning label," she teased.

Lost in the moment, she held him firmly. Her fingers barely able to touch around his girth, stroking his long, thick member, from root to tip enjoying the varying textures. He was steel wrapped in silk, both hard and smooth at the same time. Adventurously, Kai followed the thick veins with her fingertips enjoying every bump and ridge adorning his leanly muscular physique. He was an Olympian deity, strong, ripped and for the moment, he was hers.

"Shit," Aiden hissed when she rubbed her thumb over the sensitized head of his cock. Instinctively, he arched into her touch, one of his hands fitting between them, so his fingers could play with her labia. Kai stiffened briefly before letting her legs fall to the sides allowing him easier access.

Determined, Aiden continued his path down her neck with his mouth until he reached her breasts, licking one torrid peak and then its twin before finally clamping onto her throbbing nipple and pulling it more into his warm mouth. Kai felt the pull in her sex. Desperately, she clamped her legs together trying to alleviate the strong pulsing sensation of her clit, but it didn't help, only one thing would.

"Aiden?" she moaned.

"Hmm?" he mumbled, sucking her raised peak harder.

"I need...*more*," she pleaded.

Following her request, he gave her nipple one last suck before releasing it with a loud, wet pop.

"Delicious."

Finally, he continued his trek down the valley between her breasts, along her torso to her pelvic bone, where he stopped briefly to nip the skin. When he didn't move fast enough, she squeezed his cock harder to get his attention.

"Easy," he reminded with a chuckle. "I think we might need that in a few minutes."

His arrogant tone caused her to giggle like a schoolgirl. He pushed her gently backward when she tried to get up.

"Okay…no more playing around," his voice was husky. Sitting on his haunches, his gaze slid over her body admiringly. "How do you keep getting more and more beautiful, Kai?"

"Am I?" She raised her head enough to see his sex, huge and pulsing as it jutted away from his core. The head of it an angry-looking, reddish-purple, leaking pre-cum. Swallowing hard, she tried to regain the dampness in her mouth that had suddenly disappeared.

"You know you are."

Pulling her closer by her ankles, he lifted her legs and spread them farther apart, wedging his broad shoulders between them so she couldn't close them. Then he settled between her legs like he was hunkering down to read a good book.

Her face heated at his statement and his licentious position between her trembling thighs.

"You're still such a charmer."

"The last time we did…*this*, you wouldn't let me taste you…*here*."

He stroked the entrance of her pussy with his middle finger then dipped the finger inside, slowly, bypassing her wail of pleasure into her drenched heat. Soon after, another finger joined it.

"So wet, so tight…so fucking hot."

He licked his lips again as he watched his fingers plunging in and out of her pink core.

Kai shook her head.

"I did," she protested.

"Not like this, not the way I truly wanted to."

When his head lowered, Kai made no protest; didn't dare make a sound.

The moment his lips met the apex of her thighs, his tongue curling around her swollen clit, she knew she wouldn't be able to have this just once, but she couldn't wait for him to be inside her any longer. Desperation seeped into her brain, and she protested when he suddenly pulled away.

"Wait," she begged. "Don't stop."

"I have to. If not, I might explode before I even get to sample the merchandise."

He laughed when she stuck out her tongue in that impish way of hers. Teasingly, Aiden gave her clit a quick flick making her yelp. Her *kolohe*, feisty as ever.

Scooting closer until his cock was aligned with the entrance of her sex, he grasped his rock-hard member at the base and began slowly rocking his hips, notching the plump, dripping tip of his erection at her lower lips.

Kai's breath caught in her throat.

"Condom…we need…a condom."

His brow arched in shock.

"You're not on the pill?"

Adamantly, she shook her head.

Aiden gave her a quick kiss on the forehead before running toward his bathroom. He appeared a few seconds later holding a large, unopened box of extra-large condoms.

It was Kai's turn to give him a chastising glare.

"Pretty sure of yourself I see."

"A man can hope, can't he?"

Eagerly, he knelt between her still opened thighs and quickly sheathed his hard-as-nails length in two strokes.

Filled with excitement, he resumed his former position, and gave her another thought-stealing kiss, before pushing slowly into her still drenched core. Aiden's hips began the steady rocking motion from before, barely breaching her folds. Kai grabbed his shoulders, pressing her fingers into the unyielding tanned flesh. Needing to see her face, he pulled away from her lips to watch her expression as he began to work inside.

The Hawaiian goddess blew out a steady breath like she had just run a marathon.

"Holy crap!" she cried out through gritted teeth. "Did your cock get bigger since the last time we had sex?"

"It's highly unlikely," he blushed.

Another distressing whimper escaped when he propelled forward only lodging a few inches inside her channel, stretching the clamped walls of her sex as he spread her wetness along the tender tissue.

"Stop, Aiden," she winced. "I don't think I can do this."

He immediately stilled and cupped her cheek with his palm.

"You're drenched, but you're so damn tight." He lightly traced the contours of her face as he stared lovingly at her. "It's like you're still a virgin."

He grinned, but she looked away, refusing to meet his gaze.

"Kai?" He frowned as he kissed her cheek. "Talk to me. What do you normally do when this happens?"

"Nothing," she spoke so low he could barely hear her.

"C'mon." He gently took her chin in his hand, forcing her to look at him. "Don't be shy. It's me, the-pain-in-your-ass. Tell me, please."

Tears slipped past her eyes cascading down her flushed cheeks.

"This doesn't happen because I don't...I don't have sex."

Both of his brows winged up this time.

"Of course, you've had sex. Remember...six years ago, '*if you can't handle it just say so,*'" he mimicked her with his best falsetto. "Don't hurt my ego by telling me it was that forgettable."

She swallowed, hard.

"You're gorgeous and sexy," he smiled. "I'm sure you've had plenty of sex since—"

At his comment, she shook her head as her face flushed, and her eyes glistened.

"Yes, I had sex six years ago...but, I haven't since."

It was his turn to be stunned.

"What?"

"It's only been you, Aiden." She put a hand over his heart. "It's only ever been you." Kai saw the instant realization hit him like a semi-trailer.

"Kai," he soothed, carefully wiping away her tears. "Let me make it good for you."

He smiled when she pulled him down for a brief kiss.

Her chest became tight once again and she knew she was hooked.

"Do you trust me?"

The look he gave her was so tender, so sweet.

"I trust you," she nodded.

"Good," he winked. "Lay back and relax."

So, she did.

Aiden kissed his way back down her belly, nipping and licking as he went. When he reached his destination one of his hands burrowed underneath her ass, holding an entire globe in his palm, while two fingers of the other pressed to her sodden opening. Fervently, his tongue darted out and stole another taste of her labia. Following the crease of her pussy to her clit, he placed a gentle kiss on the hard bundle of nerves then slipped a third finger in her to the second knuckle.

"Hurry, Aiden," she pleaded.

"Patience."

Wrapping her hands around Aiden's head, Kai hauled him close while she bucked her hips, fucking his face with wild abandon. He consumed all of her passion in return. His primitive grunts of consent seemed to rock her to her very core, forcing his fingers to stimulate her depths. When they glided in with ease, he added a fourth, stretching her further. The tantalizing ache overwhelmed her senses, especially combined with the hummingbird-quick licks he made with his tongue against her clit.

"Holy crap!" she shrieked.

Why didn't she let him do this to her all those years ago? The man was a maestro with his tongue and hands playing her body like a well-tuned instrument.

"You are going to come for me, baby. All over my tongue. All over my face. You're going to drown me with all that sweet cream of yours."

He gave her a long swipe from slit to clit and she knew he felt a surge of triumph when she bowed off the ground chanting his name like a mantra.

"And then you're going to do it again."

He continued that wicked pace, in and out, pumping his fingers in that mind-shattering way of his. All the while licking and sucking the tiny ball of nerves. When he drew her clit into his mouth and sucked, Kai felt the orgasm hit. Her entire body burning, pulsing, and contracting. It was a miracle she didn't break Aiden's fingers.

Still, he didn't stop. As her body tried to come down off the wave of orgasmic release, Aiden continued to pump his fingers into her spasming channel, using the tip of that wicked tongue to pummel her bud with feather-like licks. When she thought she'd faint from the pure bliss, she felt another climax sneaking up. It wasn't as intense as the first, but it was still just as devastating.

When he looked up at her, eyes gleaming wickedly, face covered in the evidence of her orgasms and whispered, "One more time."

She thought she would die from overstimulation.

"No, Aiden," Kai huffed, wondering if he was trying to kill her. "I can't. It's too soon."

"One more then you'll be loose enough for me to fuck you."

Kai raised herself up onto her forearms and looked at him as if he'd lost his senses completely.

"Are you crazy?"

"Yes." He went back to work between her soaking wet thighs. "Crazy for you."

At his mercy, she leaned back as Aiden began a faster regime, pumping his four large digits into her sex while sucking her entire labia into his mouth. The dual sensation slammed another orgasm into her in less than a minute. Her mind was on overload.

"Holy crap!" she gasped breathlessly. "That feels amazing,"

Before she could enjoy the sensation of being so well satisfied, Aiden quickly rose, lined-up his cockhead to her core and began pushing inside. Kai studied his handsome face. His features were almost unrecognizable, shadowed with lust, his tanned skin taunt over high cheekbones and squared jaw. Those normally gray-blue eyes were so dark and dilated they were black, and she understood she was staring at a man who had passed the limits of his control.

Fighting his animalistic instincts, Aiden reined in his desire to plunge fully into her in one hard thrust. Every inch he penetrated was unadulterated torture, both heaven and hell. Kai's anxious, panting breaths didn't infiltrate his consciousness until he had filled her completely. From his lust-induced haze, he noticed sweat dripped from his forehead onto her cheek.

"Does it hurt?" he hissed.

"Yes, it hurts like a mother," she cried through clenched teeth. "I need you to stop playing around and move, Aiden."

With only a short withdrawal, Aiden returned to fully impale her to the hilt. Pausing at the sound of her sudden shriek, and he worried he had injured her, before realizing she was coming again with a strength he had never imagined. The clenching of her vaginal muscles drove him over the edge into his own mind-shattering release, wrenching the seed from his condom covered cock with an almost painful grip.

"Damn," he groaned, amazed by his sudden loss of control. "That hasn't happened to me in a long time."

His beautiful island flower had driven him to orgasm with just one thrust. Something that hadn't happened since he was a teenager in college. Limp from exhaustion, she groaned against his shoulder when he bent to pick her up.

"No, you sex maniac." She batted away his hands. "I can't do it again. I think my vagina is temporarily out of order."

He laughed.

"No. No more tonight…just sleep," he replied, exhausted, yet sated. "I promise."

CHAPTER FIVE

The next morning, Aiden woke to the smell of frying bacon and percolating coffee. He glanced around the small bedroom noticing Kai was no longer beside him. Contentedly, he stretched the sleep from his body, enjoying the happiness he was experiencing for the first time in a very long time. Quickly, he walked over to his closet and found a pair of sweatpants before moving to the bathroom to brush his teeth.

When he stepped into the kitchen, the sight of Kai humming and dancing as she made breakfast almost made him stumble. She looked incredible wearing one of his worn Navy t-shirts that barely covered her round, firm ass and nothing else.

"Hmm." He swept her tresses to the side and kissed the nape of her neck. She smelled of jasmine and him and sex. It was a heady combination. "Good morning, beautiful."

Kai arched her neck giving him better access.

"Good morning, sleepy head," she purred. "I didn't think you were going to wake up."

He snickered.

"Someone wore me out last night." He swatted her on the backside before going to the cabinet for two mugs. "Would you like some coffee?"

"I prefer juice in the morning," she educated with a grin.

"Ah, yes," he replied, pouring himself a cup of the heavenly scented brew. "Juice in the morning, any kind, tea at night, and mostly water during the day, right?"

"You are correct," she cooed, seemingly pleased he remembered.

He took a sip of coffee then began to set the table. Soon they were sitting down to steaming plates of pancakes, bacon, and scrambled eggs.

"In college you liked eating a big breakfast, so I decided to surprise you."

Taking a bite of his golden-brown pancake he moaned.

"This is delicious," he announced then took three more bites before looking up from his plate.

Pleased with herself, she took a bite of hers, and then smiled to herself.

"Did you go to the store for pancake mix?"

"No, I used what you had in the pantry: flour, sugar, baking powder, and a dash of salt, nothing fancy," Kai informed after a sip of juice. "Add some milk and eggs and *voile*...pancakes!"

"Good to know," he responded, making a mental note of the recipe.

Kai took a bite of her eggs and bacon before she spoke again.

"I'm surprised you didn't know that...*Mr. Food Network*." She snorted several times.

Playfully, his eyes narrowed.

"You're lucky I'm enjoying my food otherwise I'd give you that spanking I promised you last night."

"Toad," she pouted.

"Rogue." He winked playfully.

They finished their meal in relative silence, pausing once in a while to talk about what they were going to do that day. Since it was Saturday, Kai wanted to take him to the neighborhood farmer's market that sold local organic fruits and vegetables. Later, she wanted to drive up to the North

Shore to do some surfing. Knowing he was a surfer all during college, she knew he'd jump at the chance to do it again. Lastly, she wanted to have a meaningful discussion. The last part scared him a bit.

"Sounds good," he answered, gathering the dishes, and loading them into the dishwasher.

"I'll clean up since I made the mess," she stood to take over.

"Nope." He continued wiping down the countertops. "Since you cooked, I'll clean. It's fair that way."

Speechlessly, she stared at him with mock horror.

"What have you done with Aiden Kaplan?" She poked him in the back repeatedly. "Did you beam him up to your mother ship? I command you to bring him back this instant."

"Ha! Ha! Ha!" He smirked. "You're so funny."

"Yes, I am," she agreed, sticking out her tongue at him again.

"That tongue is going to get you in trouble," he warned with a smirk.

"Says who?"

"Says me," he countered.

She did it a third time, daring him to do something about it, which, of course, he did.

He lifted her chin, bending down to slant his mouth over hers. Obediently, she opened her mouth to accept him inside, tasting like fruit juice, fresh and sweet. He sucked on her tongue enjoying the hitch in her breath and the sultry moan that escaped her throat.

She whimpered when he pressed her against the counter, using his thigh to part her legs, slipping beneath the hem of the t-shirt she wore to stroke her puffy folds. She gasped when he slipped one long, thick finger into her soaking sex. Without hesitation, he released her lips to suck at a nipple through the thin cotton material hiding her gorgeous, full breasts. Lost to his ministrations, she grasped his broad shoulders when her legs began to buckle. Sensing her turmoil, Aiden lifted her onto the kitchen countertop.

"I have no control around you." He leaned his forehead against hers unable to form a coherent thought. "I want you so damn bad, Kai."

Drawing her to the edge of the countertop, he kneeled down, propped her legs over his shoulders as he covered her pussy with his mouth. He felt out of control, licking and sucking and gorging on the sweet juices that flowed from her core. He'd never felt so overwhelmed; except for the first time he had had Kai.

"I can't get enough of your sweetness, baby." He gave her one more lick before pushing two fingers into her heat. "I need you."

"I need you too," she disclosed on a whimper.

At last, he stood with a grin, pushing between her spread legs, before reaching into his sweatpants and pulling out his monster of a cock. Slowly, he entered her slick folds, inch by excruciating inch. He thought he would blackout from the sheer pleasure of being inside of her.

"Aiden," she huffed. "Don't come inside of me."

The only response he could give was a nod of his head.

"You're killing me, Kai," he gasped, pulling her hair back to gain better access to her mouth.

His entire body shuddered as he buried himself balls-deep inside of her pussy. Aiden wanted to lose control. Wanted so badly to ram himself even deeper, but he didn't want to hurt her, so he ground his teeth together and continued his slow paced entrance and withdrawal.

"Aiden!" she cried out as her body stiffened. "I'm gonna come!"

"Come for me," he moaned. "Don't hold back."

He lost control then, slamming into her like a man possessed. *Mine!* He felt that familiar tingle at the base of his spine right before his balls tightened up. A growl burst from his lungs as streams of seed spurted from his cock filling Kai's still pulsing walls. The intensity of his orgasm was so powerful his arms buckled causing him to fall onto his goddess, who was grinning like a cat who just ate a canary. For a moment, Aiden lay nestled on Kai's breasts, enjoying the tight heat surrounding his softening cock. Out of the blue, the realization hit him.

Fuck! Fuck! Fuck!

He wasn't wearing a condom.

Kai felt the last pulse of liquid heat and Aiden's cock throbbing inside of her drenched channel. She sat up from the countertop as though someone had set her on fire. Aiden stood between her legs staring down at her with a look that made her nauseous.

"Fuck!" he whispered. "I'm sorry, Kai. I'm so sorry."

She opened her mouth to speak, but nothing came out. Again, her lips parted and the words she wanted to say bubbled up inside her, but never reached the surface. This couldn't be happening.

Not again!

"Kai, please say something."

She stared up at him tears beginning to leak down her face.

"Don't worry, please don't worry." He raked a shaking hand through his sleep-mussed hair. "I've got great health insurance and there won't be any problems adding you on if…God forbid…anything should happen."

A spark suddenly appeared in the depths of her watery, amber glare.

"God forbid…is that what you said? If…God forbid, huh?" She laughed a hysterical sound that made his teeth clench. "Wow! You are some piece of work, Kaplan!"

Shit!

It was never a good sign when she called him by his last name only. It was even worse than when she called him by his full name. He slowly pulled out of her depths and put his cock back into his sweats. Knowing all too well if she had any access to the guilty body part, he'd never be able to use it again.

"Don't freak out," his voice calm and steady.

"Don't freak out, you sonofabitch!" Kai pushed him away, jumped off the counter, and bolted toward the living room, gathering her clothes as she went. Swearing and cursing under her breath. It was a mixture of English and Hawaiian and he prayed she wasn't putting a curse on him. If his junk fell off later today, he'd know why.

"Where are you going?"

She swung around to face him, pointed at him with a scowl, but didn't say anything.

"Kai, you can't leave."

He raced after her.

"We need to talk about this," he pleaded. "Don't go!"

Out of her mind, she ran towards the bathroom locking it quickly behind her. She was still fast. And she still looked sexy as hell in his t-shirt.

Damn it! Stay focused!

Gently, he knocked on the door.

"Kai, open this door. Right the hell now," he stated calmly, hoping to lure her out by using his no-nonsense military voice.

"Shove it, Kaplan!" she yelled back.

Well, that didn't work!

Note to self, do not use military voice on Kai, she's immune to it.

"Kai, we need to talk."

"Go shit in your hand, Kaplan!"

The shower came on and he wished she wasn't so pissed-off at him so he could join her. He messed up and he didn't know how to fix it. A few minutes passed before the door finally opened and Kai reemerged freshly showered wearing her clothes from the night before. Except this time, her hair was wet from her shower and hanging down her shoulders in glossy, perfect curls.

"Kai."

He grabbed her gently by the elbow before she could escape.

Defiantly, she turned, eyes puffy and red and he knew she had been crying. Bringing his hand up to his chest, he rubbed the area above his heart that began to hurt. The look in her eyes warned him not to touch her.

"You are in town for twelve weeks, is this correct?" she spoke robotically.

He stared at her blankly before responding.

"Yes."

"While you're here in Oahu, please don't call me or try to make contact with me in any way, shape, or form. If you do, I'll kill you and bury your body in my backyard." She refused to look directly at him. "Do you understand?"

"I can't make that promise, Kai," he replied. "Not seeing you would break my heart."

Her jaw was clenched, and her delicate hands balled into tight fists at her sides.

"Good," she whispered. "Because you've already broken mine."

Fueled by rage, she stepped around him, grabbed her purse from his dresser, and headed to the front door, closing it firmly behind her. Aiden stood staring at the closed door wondering what had happened to his perfect weekend.

CHAPTER SIX

The forty-five-minute drive back to Kona Cove, the subdivision where her parents lived, seemed much longer. The spring morning was picture-perfect. Azure skies decorated with wispy tropical clouds, along with the smell of pineapple and seawater calmed her ragged nerves. Like a ninja, Kai darted from her SUV into the house. Careful not to slam the front door, she quietly tried to tip-toe past her father who was chopping a myriad of colorful vegetables.

"Why are you back so soon?" her dad asked, surprised when she walked into the kitchen.

"I don't want to talk about it right now, Papa."

"Okay, no worries. How's Aiden?"

Kai shot him with a stern glare, and Joseph held up his hands in surrender.

"Sorry, didn't mean to pry."

"Why are men such idiots?" she growled, glaring at him.

"Is that a trick question?" her father gulped the nervous knot in his throat.

She stared at him again daring him to speak. Pretending to lock his mouth, he threw away the invisible key.

"I'll be in my room if you need me."

Enroute to her bedroom, she grabbed a bag of *Cool Ranch Doritos* from the pantry along with a full bag of *Oreo* cookies and several pineapple wine coolers from the fridge.

"If it's not an emergency," she mumbled. "Please, don't bother me."

Several minutes later, his wife came inside after weeding the garden.

"Is Kai here? I thought I saw her SUV parked in the driveway."

"She's here," Joseph frowned. "But she's upset and doesn't want to be disturbed."

His beautiful wife frowned too.

"Did she say why she was upset?"

"No," he replied. "But you know the look of death?"

"Of course," Leilani replied.

"She gave me one of those," he informed, shaking his head.

"I see," his wife said, removing her gloves. "I'll go talk to her."

"I wouldn't do it," Joseph glanced down at the vegetables. "Don't forget the look of death."

Leilani grinned.

"Who do you think taught her the look?"

Bang! Bang! Bang!

Marcus flipped the omelet he was cooking, lowered the heat, and raced toward the door.

"What took you so long, man?"

"Good morning to you too, sunshine," Marcus smirked at his friend.

Aiden pushed past him and went to the fridge finding the last beer hidden behind a carton of milk.

"I fucked up, big time." Aiden took a long drag of his beer. "She hates me."

"Wouldn't be the first time," Marcus smiled.

The look on Aiden's face must have convinced him of the severity of the problem.

"What did you do this time?"

At that moment, Vanessa waddled into the kitchen to check on her breakfast. The sassy mocha-complexioned, beauty looked relaxed sporting a pair of maternity overalls and a plain white t-shirt. Her dark shoulder-length hair was pulled back in a messy ponytail.

"Who hates you and why?" she questioned, placing a chaste kiss on Aiden's cheek.

Marcus answered before he could.

"Aiden was about to tell me why Kai hates him."

With some assistance from Aiden, Vanessa sat on one of the barstools as her husband handed her a very delicious smelling omelet.

"Thank you," she said grabbing her fork and digging in.

After eating half of her breakfast, she looked up, wiped her mouth and gave him a puzzled stare.

"What did you do?" she asked.

Aiden took a deep breath before answering.

"I accidentally forgot to use a condom while we were having sex this morning."

He glanced toward Marcus for support but found nothing but a shocked expression.

Vanessa cleared her throat.

"Aiden, you might have done this to her." She pointed to her extra-large stomach. "No wonder she's upset with you."

"But I didn't mean to," he explained. "We were in the throes of passion and I got carried away. She was standing in the kitchen looking defiant and sexy and lick-able, I couldn't stop myself."

He took a deep breath before he continued.

"Before I knew it...I was pumping, and she was moaning...and then I was moaning...then *Bang*! The shit hit the fan."

Vanessa shook her head, again.

"What did you say to her to make her even more upset?"

"All I said was that I have excellent health insurance if—God forbid—something happens."

The look Vanessa gave him made his balls draw-up.

"There you go," she stated matter-of-factly, refocusing on devouring the remaining omelet.

Not understanding, Aiden stared at her like she had just escaped the Looney bin.

"I still don't understand."

"She was scared," Vanessa explained. "Kai had an out of body experience and the only thing the guy who 'might' have knocked her up could say was 'I've got really good health insurance.'"

Vanessa hit him on the arm, hard.

"She probably wanted you to say you would be with her every step of the way if she were pregnant. You could have said you care about her and no matter what, she'd always have you to lean on." She picked up her fork once again. "That's what you should have said."

"Why didn't you wear a condom?" Marcus questioned his long-time buddy. "What about STD's and stuff?"

"Kai's clean," he beamed. "Believe me."

"How do you know this?" the other man glared.

"Because the last time she had sex was with me," he informed arrogantly.

Marcus's eyes bugged out of their sockets.

"You're telling me the last time Kai had sex was with you... back in college... that one time?"

"Yes," Aiden answered, wearing a broad grin.

The smack Vanessa put down on him left a bright red handprint on his arm.

"Shit!" he howled, pulling back the wounded body part. "What the hell was that for?"

"You stupid idiot!" Vanessa chastised. "She loves you!"

"What?" He shook his head. "No, she's one of my best friends. She's never once given me any signals...no you are totally off base—"

"Kai did take care of you in college, especially after your knee surgery," Marcus reminded.

"Okay, that's one thing," Aiden agreed.

"She tutored you even though she had a tough class load, plus volleyball, and working part-time."

"Good point," Aiden stated sheepishly.

"She never dated anyone in college, even though men hounded her left and right, including me," Marcus continued. "Even a couple of professors hit on her."

"Wait a minute," Aiden whispered. "You asked her out?"

"Hell yeah!" his trusted pal snapped. "Kai was gorgeous, smart, athletic, and fun...and you didn't seem interested in her that way. Although, every time someone tried to make a move on her, you were right there to cock-block."

"I did not *'cock-block'* anybody!"

"You cock-blocked me several times," Marcus smirked.

"Well, yeah, but it didn't mean anything," Aiden sighed.

Vanessa's left eye began to twitch before her husband clarified.

"Honey," he simpered. "That was way before I ever met you."

"Uh huh," she stated dryly.

Unexpectedly, Marcus slapped his forehead in mock realization.

"And on graduation day she gave *you* her virginity."

Vanessa tapped her lips, pretending to be deep in thought.

"Let's review the facts, Aiden," she stated judiciously.

"Let's," he agreed, folding his arms over his chest.

"Fact number one, Kai took care of you without you having to ask," the expectant woman began. "Fact number two, if she didn't help you through school, you probably would have flunked. Fact number three, she's never dated anyone...*ever*. Fact number four, she gave you her most prized possession...her virginity. Fact number five, she hasn't had sex with *anyone else* in six years...six long, lonely years. And finally, fact number six, she had sex with you, *again*...after six long years...*You*."

The light bulb finally clicked on in Aiden's head.

Kai was in love with him.

Well! Shit!

Knock! Knock! Knock!

"Go away. I don't want to talk about it." Kai shoved another *Oreo* into her mouth.

"Kai, it's Mama."

"I'm not in the mood for a heart-to-heart," she sighed. "Come back tomorrow."

"What did Aiden do?" her mother's muffled voice could be heard from behind the wooden barrier.

Still agitated, Kai finished chewing the *Oreo* in her mouth before letting her mom into her room.

"Nothing that I want to talk about with my mother," she stated bluntly.

"Does it deal with...*sex*?" Leilani whispered.

"Yes," Kai whispered back, and then rolled her eyes.

Leilani gave her daughter her famous *'stop-being-a-pain-in-the-butt-and-talk-to-your-mother'* look and Kai immediately shrank.

"What happened?" the other woman prodded.

"We had a great date," Kai admitted. "Aiden cooked an awesome dinner. We talked and caught up on old times...then we...you know."

"Oh, yeah...I know." Her mother waggled her eyebrows.

"Then things got out of hand, and I left," she grumbled.

"Are you going to see him again?"

"I'm not sure," Kai responded after taking a sip of her half-finished wine cooler.

"What about A.J.?"

"Of course, I'll tell him about his son...eventually. I owe him that much and he deserves to know what an incredible boy he helped make," she rambled.

"Then go back to his place and tell him," Leilani pleaded. "Now, before he finds out on his own."

She grimaced remembering their argument.

"I can't, not today."

"I never thought you'd be a coward," Leilani chastised as she stood then walked to the door with a look of disappointment that made Kai's heart clench.

"He doesn't love me, Mama," Kai sighed and reached for another cookie.

Her mother smiled.

"He does," she winked. "He just doesn't know it yet."

CHAPTER SEVEN

Lieutenant Paul Choy, Information Technology Specialist, native Hawaiian, good friend, and officer stationed at Pearl-Hickam shook his head adamantly.

"Choy," Aiden begged. "I need you to do this *one* favor for me."

"Hell, no, brah," he stated, pushing his glasses up his nose. "You're going to get me dishonorably discharged, Aiden. Plus, it's Sunday...*Sunday* my day off. I mean, it was my day off until some *haole* woke me from a very hot dream I was having featuring Kat Graham. You're also making me miss my family's weekly volleyball match."

Aiden rolled his eyes at the man he had met at Annapolis years ago.

"I wouldn't ask you to do this if I had any other choice. There are tons of Kapahu's on the island and I don't remember her parents' first names and I desperately need to find their address and phone number."

"Why didn't you find out their names before?" Paul grilled.

"Because I was in college and they were my best friend's parents, so I called them Mr. and Mrs. Kapahu...dumbass."

"Hey, be nice to me if you want my help." Paul shook his head in disbelief. "All of this for a woman?"

The other man snorted reminding Aiden of Kai.

"Must be some woman."

"She is." Aiden felt his chest tighten. "Will you help me?"

"For a price." Paul smirked then folded his arms across his chest.

Aiden's eyes narrowed while mimicking Paul's gesture.

"What price?"

"Teach me to play basketball, so I can impress the ladies." The lieutenant waggled his eyebrows.

"You don't need to be a basketball player to get women. Just be your—" Aiden rethought his words. "On the other hand, I'll teach you to play."

"Alright!" His friend did a fist pump.

Robotically turning back to face his computer, he typed some information to narrow the search parameters with the little bit of intel Aiden had provided, which was scant at best. After he had finished, he turned to Aiden with a hopeful look.

"I have the system set to send me a text message when it has the list of names."

"Thanks, Paul," he grinned. "You're a good friend."

"What are you doing today?" Paul asked.

Aiden rubbed the back of his neck trying to alleviate the stress.

"I was hoping to spend the day with the person I was telling you about," he sighed. "But that didn't work out the way I planned."

"No worries." Choy stood and grabbed his windbreaker. "You can come with me to my volleyball game."

Aiden's brows arched up.

"I don't know, man," he mumbled, already missing his woman. "I'm not the best company right now."

"Come on, *brah*," the computer wizard begged. "There's gonna be good food, cold drinks, and my Pop is baking his famous Hawaiian sweet bread."

Aiden really didn't want to go, but maybe it would take his mind off of Kai.

The other man nudged him with an elbow.

"Alright," Aiden conceded. "But I'm not driving in that deathtrap of yours. I'll follow you."

"Kai," Leilani scolded her daughter. "Fix your face. You look like someone ran over your puppy."

"It feels like it too," Kai sighed.

"Mommy! Mommy!" A.J. yelled from the parking lot adjacent to the beach where her family played volleyball every Sunday since she could remember. Her not so little bundle of joy sprinted across the sand toward her with his Uncle Koa following close behind.

"Hey, little man!"

Kai stood to catch him when he launched his small body up and into her awaiting arms, placing kisses all over his face.

"Did you miss me?" he beamed.

"More than you know," she replied, loving his sweet disposition.

"Uncle Koa and I had so much fun!" he told, his lovely gray-blue eyes sparkling in the morning sunlight.

"Yeah?" She stared at her brother's blushing face. "What did you guys do?"

Koa shook his head, his hazel eyes looking guilty.

A.J. smiled as he recalled his weekend fun.

"We went surfing!"

Kai stared at her older sibling, hard.

"You didn't take him to the Pipeline, did you?" She grimaced. "Those waves are way too big for a beginner, Koa."

Her older brother rolled his eyes.

"I know...that's why we went to Waikiki, with all the tourist, to surf the ankle-busters...small waves."

"I'm glad to hear it," she released a relieved breath.

A.J. smiled.

"We ate Spam musubi, we got shaved ice, and we picked up some *babelicious* girls—"

"You picked-up what?" Kai's smile vanished as her son's eyebrow arched.

"*Babelicious* means—"

"I know what *'babelicious'* means," Kai scoffed. "Why did you have my five-year-old picking-up women with you?"

"Nah, what had happened was—" Koa's words fell past his lips in a jumble.

"Can't you behave for a minute?" their mother admonished *her* baby boy. "You're meant to be setting a good example."

"I am setting a good example," he replied smugly. "I'm teaching him to pick-up chicks."

With that said, Kai jumped on her brother's back trying to get him in a headlock. Being a highly trained SEAL, Koa spun around, causing his sister's limbs to flail like the ribbons on a Maypole.

"Get'um, Mommy! Get'um!" A.J. jumped up and down cheering her on as she tried to wrestle her much taller and stronger brother to the ground.

"Help me, A.J.!" Kai squealed as Koa reached behind his back trying to get a hold of her.

"I got your back, Mommy!" Her little boy grabbed hold of his uncle's legs and sat on his feet, laughing loudly as his body bucked as if he were riding a rodeo bronco.

"Really?" he grinned down at his nephew. "You'd dis' me for a girl?"

A.J. nodded happily.

"Yup, that's how I roll."

"That's how you roll, huh?" Koa reached down, tickling him until he let out a squeak and let go, falling to the sand and rolling around like he was putting out a fire.

"Sorry, Mommy," he squealed, suddenly staring toward the barbeque grill Kai's dad always brought. "You're on your own."

Swiftly, he ran off in the direction of his grandmother, who was dishing up a plate of food. The boy was no fool; he knew not to miss some of his Nennie's, the name he'd started calling Kai's mom when he could barely speak, famous Sunday brunch foods.

"You're abandoning me?" Kai shouted in her son's direction.

"Yes," A.J. yelled back over his skinny shoulder.

"I gave birth to you…you little *kolohe*," she teased with mock surprise.

She knew there was no competition between her mom's macaroni and cheese and her. She'd lose every time.

In a last-ditch effort to best her brother, Kai pulled Koa's dog tags over his head and took off running at full speed across the soft sand, enjoying the feel of the rough grains between her toes. Koa was hot on her trail, swearing at her in Hawaiian. The rapidly approaching Navy SEAL made her run even faster, bobbing and weaving like her life depended on it, which if her brother caught her, she'd be in trouble.

"Give that back you little imp!" Koa was only seconds behind her, running at a steady pace.

"You're gonna have to catch me first big brother!" she yelled, giggling to herself.

However, before she could accelerate, a strong arm caught her around the waist and hauled her against a hard-as-granite chest.

"I believe that belongs to me," he chuckled holding out his hand. Koa bent his neck allowing Kai to return his dog tags to their previous position around his thick neck.

"Damn it!" Kai grasped her bikini top, trying unsuccessfully to tighten the loosened strap while holding the pretty floral material to her chest.

"What's wrong?" Koa asked, releasing her from his steely embrace.

Kai was still fidgeting with her top.

"My string is loose," she frowned.

"Turn around." Koa faced her away from him. "I'll fix it."

With deft fingers, he untied the piece of string and quickly retied it, securing it in place with a triple-knot, just in case. Turning her to face him, he held out his arms. Kai stepped into his embrace, relishing the feeling of love as he wrapped those big arms around her and for one brief moment she felt safe and happy.

"It'll all work out the way it's supposed to, little sister. It'll all work out."

And with those sweetly spoken words, Kai was pulled away from her brother's warm hug a second before Koa was tackled down to the white sand with a furious Aiden snarling on top of him.

Aiden thought his brain was going to explode. He felt the blood drain from his face at the same moment he realized the gorgeous Hawaiian beauty with curling, ebony hair, wearing a sexy black and white floral hibiscus bikini top and black shorts was Kai.

His Kai!

She was in full view, of God and everyone, horsing around with a man who resembled Dwayne *"The Rock"* Johnson and was built like a brick bunker. The two adults and a little boy were wrestling and having fun. Not showing a care in the world and what was worse…she looked happy. This Goliath-sized man made her happy.

He stared at the three in silence, completely ignoring Choy's incessant babbling about Kat Graham and *The Vampire Diaries*. He wanted to tell him to shut up, but he couldn't move a muscle. Until Kai squealed and ran off down the beach with the guy chasing after her wearing a huge grin on his way too good-looking face.

"Aiden," Paul's voice became understandable once more.

Aiden wanted to reply, but his ability to do so was currently not functioning.

"What's the matter?" the other man asked, looking in the direction he was staring at.

"What the fuck?" Aiden cursed between clenched teeth.

Paul caught sight of Kai and Koa running around like chickens with their heads cut off. His friend snorted.

"Oh, that's Kai and Koa. Don't pay them any notice. They're always like that. We're all used to it," he rambled on. "I guess it's not a Sunday brunch if someone doesn't leave with a bloody nose."

Aiden's eyes narrowed into intense slits of dangerous indigo.

"You mean they're…*together*?" He felt the bile rise in his throat.

"Hey, dude," his friend asked with a hint of confusion in his voice. "Why do you look so pissed-off?" Realization must have kicked in.

"Oh…*Oh, damn!* She's the best friend from college?!" Paul proclaimed.

"I'm gonna kill him!"

"Shit! Aiden, wait! It's not what you think!" Paul shouted at the quickly moving man. "I guess we won't need that spreadsheet anymore. You're welcome!"

Aiden took off at full speed after the two people. His best friend and the man who was soon to have his ass kicked, who were currently running down the almost-empty beach. They disappeared briefly, but when Aiden located them again, the man was undoing her bikini top. Right out in the open.

Fuck that shit!

His vision blurred with rage as he pulled Kai out of the big Hawaiian's arms and started swinging.

"Aiden, damn it, you moron!" Kai screeched. "Get the hell off of him!"

"What the…" Koa's head snapped back as Aiden's fist caught him on the jaw.

Desperation fueled her actions as she lunged on top of Aiden trying to pry off the two-hundred-and-twenty-pound wall of a man, currently pounding into her brother.

"Stop it! Aiden… please stop!" she sobbed loudly; voice unrecognizable.

With a movement almost too fast to discern, Koa threw his opponent off of him and pinned the other man down in a full nelson. To her amazement, Aiden did a countermove that temporarily loosened her brother's grip and twisted his own body up to a standing position. He lunged for Koa again, this time landing a punch to his gut. Koa grunted from the impact and stumbled back a few inches before regaining his balance on the shifting sand beneath him.

"Koa, don't hurt him!" Kai yelled at the top of her voice. Her brother must not have heard her because he punched Aiden directly in the kidneys, making him fall grasping the injured area. "Don't hurt him, damn it!"

"He attacked me first!" Koa hissed getting ready to attack Aiden once more.

Desperately, Kai grabbed his arm.

"This is Aiden! He's Aiden!"

Koa's eyebrow lifted almost to his hairline. Deep in thought, he looked down at the outstretched man then back up to his sister. His eyes widened in disbelief.

"Sorry, my bad." The highly-trained warrior snapped back to his regular playful, fun-loving self and out of combat mode, then offered the other man his hand to help him up.

Temporarily stunned into silence, Aiden lay on the ground looking up at the offered hand debating if he should hit him again.

"Aiden," Kai's eyes were wide with worry. "This is Koa... he's my brother."

Without animosity, Koa reached down to pull the other man up, chuckling like it was a big game.

"Well, well, well," Koa glanced over at Kai. "So, this is the infamous Aiden Kaplan."

Kai shook her head as her brother laughed a full belly laugh that eased his tension.

"Nice to meet ya, *brah*." Koa shook his hand and winked at his sister. "I'm gonna leave you two to talk. I'm hungry."

Playfully, he kissed Kai's cheek before patting Aiden on the shoulder.

"I guess I'll be seeing *you* around."

Quickly, Koa turned and walked back toward the gathering still rubbing his jaw.

"Are you okay?" Kai asked, slowly moving toward a still very angry-looking Aiden.

Wary of his current state of agitation, she stopped a few inches in front of him wanting to touch him, but not knowing if she should. *Wasn't she supposed to be upset with him?* Before she could make up her mind, he reached out, grabbed her gently by the wrist and pulled her against his hard chest.

Burying his head at the side of her neck, she felt him inhale deeply and then kiss her tenderly below the earlobe. Needing to be closer, she wound her arms around his neck and pulled his lips down to her awaiting mouth.

"I'm sorry, baby," he whispered against her lips. "I never meant to hurt you...never."

Tenderly, he secured his lips to hers. The gentle act causing an ache in her soul. The heat from his cotton-covered chest warming her from the inside out as he crushed her breasts, making it difficult to think clearly. Suddenly, she felt needy and complete at the same time.

Kai whimpered into his mouth, tasting the wicked lashes of his knowledgeable tongue as he licked and nipped at her kiss-swollen lips. Ravaging them with the sweetest form of punishment. The man stole her heart with every press of his lips and she doubted he knew how much he affected her.

Unexpectedly, he groaned loudly, still pressing against her mouth. His hands now buried deep beneath her hair holding her nape securely. Aiden released her mouth briefly, inhaled a quick breath then resumed his position over her lips once more.

Something hard moved against her and she realized it was his erection pressing against the front of her hip. He pumped the growing appendage slowly against her as he continued the assault inside her mouth. If he didn't stop now, she'd take him inside her, right here, right now...to hell with the consequences.

Somehow, she found the strength to pull away a few inches. He looked at her with such longing she couldn't breathe again.

"Aiden, please stop," she pleaded.

"I don't think I can," he whispered. "I need you. Let's go."

"I can't," she sighed.

"Come on, we'll go back to my place."

"No, I need to tell you something...something very important," she insisted.

"Okay," he sighed. "What is it?"

"Mommy?"

A small voice caught her attention, and Kai looked down to see her son, staring at her with his eyebrows highly arched.

"What are you doing?"

For a moment, Aiden thought he'd misheard until Kai answered the little boy who stood looking up at him with familiar gray-blue eyes.

"Mommy is just talking to her friend," she cleared her throat. "Remember the one I went out on a date with?"

"Oh, yeah," the boy replied, smiling up at him.

Aiden smiled back, temporarily releasing Kai to speak to him.

"Hello."

"*Aloha*," the boy responded with a cute Hawaiian lilt to his voice and offered him his hand. "I'm A.J. Kapahu,"

Aiden shook the boy's hand and grinned at his good manners.

"Hello, A.J.," Aiden repeated. "My name is Aiden…Aiden Kaplan."

The boy's eyebrows arched and Aiden felt a funny tightening in his stomach.

"That's my name too," A.J. informed matter-of-factly.

Aiden looked over at Kai, who stood with her eyes closed, hands tightly grasped together. The boy didn't seem to notice the sick look she seemed to be wearing over her beautiful face.

"The food is getting cold, Mommy," he reminded. "Nennie said to come and get some while it's still hot."

"Okay." Kai shivered although it had to be at least eighty degrees. "Tell her I'll be right there."

A.J. looked at her strangely then back up at him. The boy's eyes changing to a clear sky-blue.

"Mr. Kaplan, are you staying for lunch?" A.J. asked. "We have a lot of good stuff...hamburgers, hot dogs, chicken wings, macaroni and cheese—"

"A.J.," Kai interrupted his list. "I have to talk with my friend, okay? I'll see you in a bit."

"Ok," her son winked. "It was nice meeting you, sir."

"It was nice meeting you too, A.J."

Aiden felt his head begin to spin before Kai grabbed his elbow and helped him sit in the sand with his head tucked between his knees. She sat beside him, their thighs pressing together.

"Why didn't you tell me I have a son, Kai?" his voice was void of emotion.

"I tried to," she whispered on the verge of tears. "I found out six weeks after we...you know." She sniffled. "When I was positive I was pregnant I called you. I called you every day for a whole month. I left messages on your cell phone, hundreds of them, b-but you never called me back. So then I started sending letters to your dad's house. They were all returned unopened. I still have them at home."

Her tears were freely falling now, but Aiden refused to touch her.

"My last resort was tracking down your father at Annapolis so he could tell you what was happening, but I guess he never gave you the message," Kai stated dryly.

"But we used a condom," he muttered, still looking pale.

"Obviously, it didn't work," she replied meekly.

"But that's what it's meant to do...*to work*...its only purpose, damn it...is to work," he rambled.

"If you still have the receipt, you can go back to the store and get your money back," she poked sarcastically.

"Smartass," he said without heat. Her pain was more than he could bear. Gently, he took her hands in his and stroked the smooth skin of her wrist with his fingers, trying to comfort her. "Why didn't you tell me at the hospital?"

Aiden turned to face her.

She sighed.

"I was angry with you," she responded without heat. "You abandoned me, and we were supposed to be best friends, but you forgot about me the minute you left USC."

Filled with shame, he shook his head.

"I never forgot about you, even though, I tried really hard to. Why do you think I've only had one girlfriend since college?"

Kai leaned her head on his shoulder and smirked.

"Because you're a beast who should be locked in a dungeon somewhere?"

"Harpy," he ribbed.

Finally, she smiled.

"Savage."

Unable to resist any longer, he pulled her into his lap, trying to stroke her wild curls into submission without success.

"No, because I couldn't stop thinking about my little Hawaiian flower who drove me crazy with her sharp tongue, her tendency for violence, and her ability to keep me on my toes," he replied with a grunt to ease the strain between them. "I started comparing every woman I met to her and they all came up wanting."

She smiled at him, amber eyes glistening.

"How's this going to work?" Aiden asked.

"I don't know?" She tensed again. "I don't know how to tell my son…I mean our son that you're his father? I don't know how he's going to take it."

"We'll figure it out," he comforted.

"Hopefully."

Kai stared out towards the vast Pacific wishing she could lose herself in it.

Suddenly, Aiden stood bringing her up with him.

"Let's get some food."

The entire Kapahu clan was staring at them when they joined the festivities.

"Everything alright, Kai?" Mrs. Kapahu asked as they joined the rest of Kai's family already sitting at picnic tables and blankets enjoying their food.

Aiden's stomach growled reminding him he hadn't eaten all morning.

"So far, so good," she replied in a hushed tone.

Mrs. Kapahu gave him a big hug and pointed him in the direction of the food.

"You're still too skinny, Aiden," she teased. "I'll have to fatten you up."

"He's perfect just the way he is," Kai's words crept out of her mouth before she could stop them; her eyes widening at the realization she had spoken them aloud.

Aiden chuckled at her embarrassment.

Just too damn cute for her own good.

"Kai, fix Aiden a plate," her mom encouraged.

"Why? He's got two good hands." She handed him a disposable plate and plastic silverware wrapped in a white paper napkin. She giggled when he stuck his tongue out at her.

"Mr. Kaplan." A.J. ran up behind them and tugged on Aiden's t-shirt. "Do you want to play volleyball after you eat?"

"Sure," Aiden replied with a smile. "But I have to warn you, I'm not very good at volleyball. Basketball is more my sport or surfing."

"You surf?" A.J.'s eyes widened with surprise.

"Yup." Aiden winked. "I'm pretty good too."

"Uncle Koa is teaching me how to hang-ten." A.J. pretended to balance on an invisible surfboard. "Maybe, you can come with us sometime?"

He couldn't help smiling.

"I'd like that. You can show me your moves."

"Cool. I'll tell Uncle Koa." The little boy turned and ran back toward the rest of the kids.

"I think he likes you." Kai chuckled when their son began dancing around Koa's feet, talking and waving his hands around animatedly.

They finished filling their plates and went to sit at a table several feet away from the rest of the family. Aiden ate while watching Kai relish each bite of her assortment of goodies. He grinned when she went back for a second helping. He liked a female with a healthy appetite, one that didn't order a salad at a restaurant, ate half then pretended to be full. It drove him crazy.

He snickered when she took a big bite of her grilled chicken.

"What?" She rolled her eyes at him. "I'm starving. I've only eaten cookies and chips during the last twenty-four hours."

Her admission made him frown knowing those were her go-to-foods when she was upset. Often during their time at university, he'd walked into her dorm room only to find her gorging herself on *Double-Stuffed Oreos* and a wide variety of chips. When she was really angry, she'd wash it all down with wine coolers. Aiden realized now she only performed this particular ritual when she was upset with something he had done or said. How could he have been so blind?

"You're staring," Kai snickered below her breath.

"You have a little barbeque sauce on the corner of your mouth."

He unconsciously licked his own lips.

"I could lick it off of you," he taunted, slowly leaning towards her.

She laughed, holding him at arm's length.

"Stop that!" she whispered. "A.J. is right over there."

"So?"

"So, you have to act like an adult instead of a pig."

She used her napkin to wipe her mouth taking the temptation out of his way.

Still in shock, he blinked at the idea that he was a father.

"He seems like a great kid," he flattered sincerely. "Does A.J. stand for Aiden Junior?"

Kai shook her head and he felt a pang of disappointment.

"It stands for Aiden Joseph. He's not a junior because he doesn't have your last name," she said without animosity, which surprised him. "Since you and my dad share the same name, I thought it fitting."

"You didn't put my name on the birth certificate?" he cautiously asked.

She stared at him for a moment before answering.

"Of course, I put your name on his birth certificate," she stated firmly. "I just didn't want to make the assumption you'd want him to have your last name. For all I knew, your father had told you about the pregnancy and you just didn't care."

Those words put their whole relationship in perspective. Kai did not trust him and rightly so. She had been a single parent at twenty-three, having to be both mother and father to their son. Thank goodness she had the support of a loving family, something he hadn't had since his mother's death.

When his mom died in a car crash when he was a teenager, his father buried himself in his career and never climbed back out. He left his son in the care of nannies, housekeepers, and cooks while he traveled the world on his aircraft carrier with his crew of sailors.

Until now, Aiden didn't hold it against the man. He figured that was just the way it was. He had thirteen years filled with good memories of both his mom and dad and he was fine with that. However, knowing now his father knew he had a grandson in Hawaii who needed a dad was the straw that broke the camel's back. Tonight, he'd call up the man who *he* called dad and tear him a new one.

"Mr. Kaplan?" A.J. was suddenly standing next to his elbow. *The kid was as fast as his mother.* "We're getting ready to start the volleyball game. Are you playing?"

"Definitely, I'll be right there," Aiden replied.

"Okay." He ran back over to the group gathering by the volleyball net.

"Kai, you're playing too, right?" he asked as he pulled her away from the table.

"Sure," she said haughtily. "I'll kick your butt for old time's sake,"

Happily, Aiden held her hand and led her toward the court.

"We'll see about that…"

CHAPTER EIGHT

"Kai, you look fabulous!" Aiden complimented.

His heated stare and appreciative wide-mouthed gape made her blush. When she looked down shyly, he turned to their son for their now traditional fist bump and hug.

Even though the three of them were spending a lot of time together she still wanted it to be memorable. Tonight, she took her time picking out her clothes, wanting to look extra nice for *both* of her men. Although, she couldn't say for certain she could claim Aiden as her own…yet. She'd have to wait and see.

Her final choice for this outing was a plain black, knee-length, sleeveless sheath dress with a conservative neckline that still accented her curves. She took almost an hour with her *Sedu*, straightening her curls until her hair fell past her shoulders in soft layers. On her feet, a pair of black, flat, peek-a-boo ballet slippers. Her makeup she also took a little time with. Applying smoky eye shadow, eyeliner and mascara which made her bright amber eyes look even brighter, but her lipstick was the same nude gloss that she liked. The only jewelry she wore was a thin, yellow-gold necklace with a black pearl charm, and from the way Aiden kept staring at her, she had made the right choices.

"*Mahalo*," Kai replied trying to keep her composure. "You look very handsome too."

And he did… really did. His outfit was casual, but still very sexy. Dark-washed jeans, a cerulean button-down dress shirt that enhanced his eyes, black blazer, the platinum *Tag Heuer* watch he had gotten as a gift and black sneakers.

"A.J.," he spoke while kneeling down to see him, blue eyes to blue eyes. "You look very nice as well."

"Thank you," his son grinned, showing off the new space where his front tooth used to be. "I picked out my own clothes."

A.J. had also done an excellent job picking out his clothes for their third dinner together that week. Their son wore dark jeans, a white polo, and white sneakers.

"He asked me to spike his hair for a more *fashionable* look," she added with a wink.

Kai had worked late, so their dinner date was a little later than usual, but it was Friday, so it wasn't a problem. They met at the restaurant, a fun new place with a live reggae band and a dance floor that was also kid friendly. An eager waiter took their food orders shortly after they were seated, salmon for Aiden, chicken fingers for A.J., and pasta for her.

"I like this place," Kai told, breaking their comfortable silence.

"Yeah." His gaze swept the room. "It's laid-back and not too crowded."

Appreciatively, she rested her hand over Aiden's, enjoying the ease their trio seemed to have fallen into. Sometimes it was easy to forget Aiden wouldn't be around forever. Just another ten weeks.

A.J. giggled.

"What's so funny, little man?" Aiden's left brow rose, but he was grinning.

"Nothing." The little boy giggled again.

"Are you sure?" he poked again.

"Sir, yes, sir," A.J. mimicked his Uncle Koa, making them all chuckle.

Their drinks arrived while Aiden was telling them about his day rewiring a faulty underwater electrical transponder. A.J. was riveted, asking questions one after another, and she worried Aiden would feel overwhelmed.

Sometimes their son overwhelmed her, but Aiden always went out of his way to explain, clarify, or expound when necessary. As Kai sat enthralled by their conversation, she couldn't help wondering if A.J. would follow in his father's footsteps and become an engineer as well. The thought made her smile.

From his expression, Aiden seemed to be quite entranced with his son, smiling and nodding when the precocious five-year-old entertained him with stories of his friend, Bruce. And how said friend accidentally shot apple juice out of his noise during lunch or when a girl named, Karen, yelled at his friend, Jonathan, when he sneezed without covering his mouth. She had met Karen's mom, Linda, and wasn't surprised the little girl was a germaphobe as well.

She grinned when Aiden explained the merits of covering your mouth and nose when you sneeze. A.J. agreed after all of the facts were presented. Making Kai extremely happy the little boy would work a bit harder to comply with Aiden's newly given facts about the spreading of germs.

"Monday, when you see Bruce at school, let him know it's better to sneeze into your elbow or a tissue. Oh," Aiden suggested. "And let him know not to wipe his nose on his sleeve anymore. It's just unsanitary."

A.J. shook his head in agreement and she had to bite her lower lip in order not to belly laugh.

"Wait a minute," Aiden announced suddenly. "This is one of your mom's favorite songs."

Kai listened carefully as the band began to play *Bob Marley's Is This Love*. Her mouth dropped at the fact he had remembered her favorite song after all those years. She felt that tingle in her stomach and the sweat beading on her upper lip.

Wow! He was simply...Amazing!

Slowly, Aiden stood and offered his hand.

"Dance with me." It wasn't a question.

Kai frowned.

"As I recall you can't dance."

The man smiled one of his patented panty soakers and she felt her heart begin to pound inside her chest. So hard in fact, she thought he could hear how much he affected her.

"I never said I couldn't dance," he declared with a cheeky smirk. "I just let you think that."

"Why?" she probed, curiosity getting the best of her.

"Because I didn't think I could be that close to you without trying to kiss you," he informed with reddened cheeks. "And I didn't want you to beat me up."

A.J. laughed and Aiden raised his brow at him.

"You're dancing too," he added matter-of-factly. "Let's go."

Happy to oblige, their son got up and followed them to the dance floor.

"How are we going to do this? Her brow furrowed, unable to imagine how the three of them were going to dance, together.

"You'll see."

Aiden instructed A.J. to place each of his feet on top of his and hold on to his legs. Next, he pulled Kai into his embrace being careful not to crush A.J. in the process. Slowly they moved, barely swaying back and forth to the beat of the song. It was the happiest moment she'd experienced in a long time.

Kai loved that he was so patient with A.J. She loved that he was trying so hard to get to know their son. But most of all, she loved him.

"I can't believe he fell asleep so fast," she confessed. "He's usually out of bed at least twice before falling asleep, asking for a drink of water or for me to check inside his closet and under the bed for monsters."

Aiden smiled as he watched his son tucked in bed. The *Superman* comforter was pulled up to his neck and tucked tightly under his small body, so he looked like a mummy.

"Isn't he going to be hot like that?"

"We saw the movie *The Little Vampire* on the Disney Channel last month and he sleeps like this now so it's more difficult for him to get bitten," Kai whispered.

At this new information, Aiden almost burst out laughing, biting the inside of his cheek so he wouldn't wake A.J. Kai followed him out of the bedroom. Gently, closing the door behind them, and then pulled him into her bedroom located across the hall.

As soon as the door was closed, she pushed him against the wooden surface. As usual, he felt his cock begin to grow. Without a word, she tiptoed, smashing their chests together right before pulling his mouth down to hers, barely a centimeter separating them. The fragrance of jasmine infiltrated his senses, forcing all reasonable thought out of his mind.

"I'm gonna kiss you now," she informed seductively, licking her bottom lip.

"It's about time." His muscular arms encircled her waist in a tight grip before stating, "I've been waiting for you to kiss me all night."

"Why didn't you kiss me first?" she feigned annoyance.

"I was behaving myself in front of my son, unlike some people I know," he teased. "Wasn't it your hand on my thigh during dinner?"

"Cyclops," she hissed with a naughty grin.

"Old maid," he retorted dryly, but couldn't keep a straight face.

"What did you call me?" Her eyes twinkled in the dimly lit room.

He chuckled.

"Have I told you lately how beautiful you are?"

Her shy, girlish smile made his heartbeat accelerate.

"Not within the last couple of hours," she replied, voice low and raspy.

"Why do you have to be so...*you*?" he questioned, rolling his eyes.

Kai opened her mouth to protest but was quickly silenced by Aiden's lips. He claimed her mouth...hard. Forcing her to give him entrance into the sweetness he couldn't get enough of. Expertly, his tongue dueled with hers, lashing against each other like swordfighters parrying and thrusting, mimicking a rhythm they'd soon be recreating with their bodies.

Unable to be rational, he pulled away first, unable to think of anything else except getting inside of her hot, wet sex.

"What are you doing to me?"

He traced a line with the tip of his tongue from her ear to her collarbone.

"I've never felt this out of control. This obsessed," he admitted. "You've put a spell on me, Kai Kapahu, and now I'm yours."

"*Mmm*," was her only reply. "I guess I'm just naughty that way."

Impatient hands moved away from her waist, gliding slowly up and down her body, caressing each delicious, womanly curve that was his Kai. Even through the thin material of her dress, her body felt exquisite. Feminine. And she was his. Of that, he had no doubt.

Powerless to stop himself, he kissed her again. This time it was a slow, desperate glide that made her moan into his mouth. The needy vibration traveled down his spine and into his balls. "How thick are these walls?" he whispered while trying to catch his breath when their lips finally parted.

"Not very... thick," she replied almost too weak to hear.

"Shit!" His hands were slowly traveling down her shoulders, over her hips, then around to her ass. "We haven't had sex in almost a week."

"Didn't you tell me you hadn't had sex in over two years before last Friday?" she commented.

"That doesn't matter," he insisted, squeezing the firm glutes with his palms, enjoying the way it made her squirm.

"Why doesn't it matter?" she interrogated on a muffled gasp.

Leaving his right hand on her butt, he moved his left one up to push aside her hair, before starting to slowly kiss and suck on the exposed flesh of her neck.

"Because now I'm having sex again...with you...I can't stop thinking about us...having sex...all of the time." He cemented his words with a grind of his pelvis knowing she would feel the evidence of his arousal.

"Really?" she gasped as his cock hardened even more.

"Uh huh," he groaned, unable to express himself in any other way at the moment. Aiden was losing his mind as he pumped his hips against her, the denim now an annoying barrier.

"I want to have you on every flat surface of my apartment, in my car, on my desk...under my desk."

Wickedly, he sucked her earlobe into his mouth, fascinated by the way it caused her to rock into him.

"Pig," she sighed against his cheek.

She reached around and squeezed his ass.

"My cock's so damn stiff I don't think I can walk to the car right now," he confessed. His movement becoming more frantic. More desperate. "I need you."

"I don't know, Aiden. My parents are in their room and A.J. is next door. It just feels—"

"Scandalous," he teased. "Have I scandalized you?"

"I think you did that when you knocked me up," she whispered.

Quickly, he turned them around, so she was now leaning against the door, before dropping to his knees. His hands immediately traveled under her dress, caressing the long-toned legs hiding beneath.

"I've always loved your legs," he complimented as he continued his upward journey from her calves, past her knees, over her thighs until his hands were resting over her damp, plump lace-covered mound.

"I didn't know," she panted.

His mind went blank as he began rubbing slow circles over her lower lips with his thumbs. He felt dizzy with lust.

"You're so wet already," his voice was a fascinated whisper.

"Aiden, please stop teasing me," her raspy voice sounded like a plea.

Grabbing the sides of her black lace panties, he pulled them slowly down to her ankles.

"Step out," he commanded.

When the strip of fabric was off, he slid his hands back to the apex of her thighs. Before she could protest, he sunk two thick digits inside. Thrusting in an unhurried rhythm into her very slick entrance while using his thumb to circle her clit once more, giving her no quarter. Forcing her to accept whatever he gave her.

"Aiden," his name escaped her on a moan. "If you don't stop playing around, I'm gonna have to kill you."

He laughed against her damp inner thigh.

"Can't you ever be patient?"

"Can't you ever *not* be an ass?"

Ignoring her insult, he continued his movements relishing the way Kai's body responded to his touch. Her breath hitching on silent moans, hands grasping and tugging at his shortly cropped hair. Those sexy legs began shaking as the climax built inside of her, pulling her into a vortex of ecstasy.

"*Ahhh*... Aiden," she whimpered, rocking her pelvis against his hand. He didn't know how much more he could take before coming in his pants.

"Kai, baby," he gasped as her pussy walls began to contract against his fingers in that mind-blowing way. "Baby, I need you to come. Now, before I explode."

The orgasm hit her hard as her whole body shuddered violently then stilled, breath coming in hard, needy gasps.

"Hold this," he said while shoving her dress up around her waist.

She did as she was told without complaint, or in Kai's case, without argument.

"I need you," she moaned, features strained with desire.

Desperately, he kissed a trail from mid-thigh up to her sex, placing a kiss to her glistening lower lips. "Spread these gorgeous legs for me."

Aiden stopped momentarily to fish a condom from his back pocket, quickly donning the latex sheath over his massive member.

Kai stared down at him watching his movements curiously.

"Hurry."

He stood suddenly, pushing her more securely against the now locked door.

"Don't let go of your dress," he commanded, dusky eyes glimmering even in the darkened room.

Then he was inside her with one hard thrust. He felt her stiffen and saw when she squeezed her eyes shut.

"Look at me, baby," he commanded, voice thick with yearning. "I want to see you when you come again."

Kai opened her eyes at his request, anxiety hardening her features.

"Am I hurting you?"

She shook her head.

"A.J. might hear us," her voice was breathless. "Or my parents—"

"Shh," he begged, before kissing the tip of her nose. "Just feel what I'm doing to you. Feel me inside your tight, soaked pussy."

His breathing was erratic and strained.

"I want you to feel me explode inside of you."

She did as she was told, feeling surprisingly aroused by his forceful bedroom manner.

"Aiden," she whispered his name like a prayer.

Like a sex-crazed teenager, he pumped in and out of her wet channel while raining kisses down her neck. Unable to do anything else except stand and take what he gave, Kai held her skirt tight in her hands as the sensual force of nature, which was Aiden Kaplan, thrust deep inside of her. She thought she might faint from the pleasure of it. Barely noticing she was balancing on her tiptoes, pressed between the rattling door and a rock-hard, determined man pistoning wildly into her sex. Needing her to come, he reached between their bodies finding the sensitive bundle of nerves at the top of her thighs and began rubbing it gently with the pad of his thumb.

"Holy crap, Aiden!" she whimpered, feeling her legs beginning to shake as another orgasm threatened to hit.

Squeezing his eyes shut he growled, "You're killing me, Kai."

"Close...so damn close...don't stop." Tears of ecstasy welled in her amber depths. "Aiden?"

"Yes," his voice strained.

"Is it always like this?" she moaned.

Aiden shook his head.

"No...never...it's only ever felt like this with you."

It was the truth. Kai was so innocent, yet she could seduce him with only a bat of her eyes or the sway of her hips. Her melodious voice with that exotic Hawaiian lilt was the last sound he wanted to hear before falling asleep and the first thing he wanted to hear when he awoke. She was a siren, luring him into uncharted waters, unable to guide himself back to his once uneventful life.

Mesmerized by everything about her, Aiden watched her watching him and the epiphany hit him like a lightning bolt. Kai was perfect for him. Beautiful, sexy, smart, and a terrific mother to his child. She made him believe he could do anything he set his mind to, and she never judged him when he messed up. And he knew he messed up often. She was his lover and his best friend, and he couldn't see himself with anyone else. He loved her. With every fiber of his being, he loved her and that was never going to change.

"I'm not going to last very much longer, baby," Aiden hissed through clenched teeth. "Come for me."

That one firm command was all it took to send her careening over the cliff. Her body stiffened with the force of her orgasm. He felt a surge of pride engulf him when a satisfied purr escaped her lips. The tight contractions of her internal muscles causing him to find his release as well.

It was all too much. With the feeling of contentment washing over him, Aiden couldn't hold his emotions back any longer.

"I love you, Kai," he said in a hushed whisper.

His cock still pulsed inside her filling the condom with his seed.

"I love you so fucking much."

Kai tried to be silent, tried to analyze the words Aiden had just proclaimed a few moments before.

I love you, Kai.

Four little words she had longed to hear, but she couldn't trust his proclamation wasn't uttered in a moment of mindless passion. No. She couldn't take those words at face value.

Not yet.

Somehow, they had moved to her queen-sized bed when their legs had stopped wobbling. Content to be cradled in his arms, her head secured in the crook of his neck, breathing in their combined scent of musk and jasmine and sex. It was intoxicating.

"We're practically fully dressed." She giggled as her brain finally kicked into gear after their passionate love-making.

"Hmm." Aiden lay, eyes closed, a smug grin pasted onto his rugged features, a slight flush adorning his cheeks.

"What are you thinking about?" she asked as her fingers traced his rugged jaw line.

"You," he answered.

"What are you thinking about me?" Her interest now piqued.

"How much I love you…and A.J."

His words were like a punch to the gut.

"How do you know?" she prodded. "Suppose it's just the aftereffects of great sex."

"Silly girl," he laughed. "I think I've loved you since the day you yelled at me for making a dent in your textbook with my 'Cro-Magnon cranium' then stepped over me like I was a piece of gum that would stick to the bottom of your shoes."

She laughed too.

"Don't laugh," he chastised. "I might have had a concussion."

She laughed louder.

"Shh," he reprimanded with mock indignation. "You're going to wake up *our* son."

Kai snickered, enjoying his playfulness.

"That physics book was over a hundred dollars. Not everyone has a rich daddy you know."

Pulling her closer, he placed a quick, chaste kiss to her temple, eyes still closed.

"Aiden?"

"Yes, my love."

"I love you too."

He snuggled closer.

"I know…I know."

Then she drifted off to sleep.

❦

Knock! Knock! Knock!

"Mommy?"

A soft voice came from outside Kai's bedroom door. Aiden blinked trying to get his eyes to focus. The alarm clock claimed it was six thirty in the morning.

"Mommy, may I sleep with you?"

Oh shit!

A sudden rush of panic streaked through his veins, making his head spin and his palms sweat.

"Kai," he whispered. "*Kai*…damn it, wake-up."

Half asleep, she groaned and pulled the covers over her head. Not knowing what else to do, he pinched her arm hard.

"Ouch! That hurt!" She sat up suddenly, pinching him back. "What are you doing?!"

Aiden nodded toward the locked door.

"A.J. w-wants to c-come in," he stammered, feeling the bile rising in his throat.

"Damn it!" she mouthed.

Horrified at their child seeing them like *this*, Kai jumped out of bed. Thank goodness she was still wearing the dress she wore the night before *sans* panties. He grinned remembering their night of passion. A smile crept over his face.

"Stop thinking about sex and hide in the closet," she commanded in a low tone, a worried look on her face.

"What?" he whispered.

"Hide in the closet until he falls back to sleep," she demanded. "Then you can sneak out of the house and come back later for breakfast."

"Mommy, are you awake?" A.J. wiggled the doorknob.

"Shit!" he mouthed back.

This was not how he wanted his son to see him, disheveled, in his mother's bedroom, smelling of sex and looking guilty.

"One-minute, little man!" she yelled, still unable to clear the cobwebs from her sleep drenched brain.

"Kai?!"

"Hurry, get in the closet," she commanded again in that same hushed tone.

Hastily, he ran into the small walk-in closet and gently shut the door. Kai must have opened the bedroom door because he heard A.J.'s voice much closer this time.

"What took you so long, Mommy?"

"Sorry," she replied clearly. "Mommy was just having a very pleasant dream."

Aiden smiled to himself.

"Oh," A.J. yawned. "May I sleep with you?"

"Sure, hop in. Just don't steal the covers," she joked.

The sound of his son's innocent giggle followed by his mother's sleep-laced laugh caused that now familiar clenching in his heart again, but instead of it terrifying him, it made him smile. He finally understood that the sun rose and fell because of the two people on the other side of the closet door, and he loved them even more.

Mine.

Bored out of his mind, Aiden sat in the closet for a little over thirty minutes before daring to peek into the bedroom. The sight that met him made him smile. Kai and A.J. were fast asleep, Kai snoring lightly. He'd have to remember to tease her about it later.

Quietly, he tiptoed out of the room, his sneakers in hand, and made a run to the front door.

"Morning, Aiden." Mr. Kapahu sat at the dining table drinking a glass of grapefruit juice and reading the morning paper. "I was wondering when you were going to make a run for it." The older man smirked.

"Sorry, Mr. Kapahu," he blushed. "I didn't mean to stay overnight, but I accidentally…fell asleep."

Aiden glanced around nervously.

Mr. Kapahu waved him over, motioned for him to sit down and then poured him a glass of juice.

"Are Kai and A.J. still asleep?"

"Yes, sir," he gulped.

Mr. Kapahu laughed.

"It'll probably be another couple of hours before they wake up, so you might as well go get cleaned up."

Aiden's eyes widened.

"Pardon me?"

"Koa's old bedroom is still as he left it, sometimes he sleeps over," the gentle giant nodded in the direction. "He's got some clothes that might fit you."

Aiden drank his juice quickly as the other man watched him with a knowing look on his much darker face.

"Mr. Kapahu," Aiden cleared his throat. "I love your daughter and our son, and I just wanted to let you know my intention is to be with them always. And if you give me your blessing, I'd like to ask Kai to marry me."

The man's brow arched and the same scrutinizing gaze that often-marred Kai's face appeared. Aiden gulped at the intensity of his stare.

"If I don't give you my blessing, will you still ask her to marry you?"

"Yes," he answered without hesitation. "I'm claiming Kai."

There was a long pause as Aiden held his breath, lungs threatening to burst as he waited for her father's response.

"Good," Mr. Kapahu encouraged with a broad smile. "Then go get showered. There are clean towels in the linen closet and new toothbrushes under the sink in the guest bathroom at the end of the hall."

"Thank you."

Relief filled him as he stood to leave the room.

"Aiden?"

"Yes, sir?"

Mr. Kapahu smirked once more.

"Make sure you wash really well...you stink."

Aiden felt all the blood drain from his face as he bolted towards Koa's room.

Shit!

Not a great way to impress your future father-in-law.

"Good morning, sleepy heads," Aiden greeted the love of his life and his son.

Kai's brow rose before she walked over to grace him with a kiss to the cheek.

"When did you get back?"

"I never left," Aiden whispered.

"Where did you get the clean clothes?"

He blushed.

"They're Koa's."

After his shower, he had gone rummaging through Koa's closet and found a pair of dark gray sweatpants and matching t-shirt. They were a little baggy and long, but they were clean and comfortable.

This time both brows hitched upward.

"Huh," she stated flatly.

Without another word, she went to grab a glass, mug, and a plastic kiddy cup from the cupboard.

"Want some coffee?" Kai asked.

"Yes, please."

"Aloha, Mr. Kaplan!"

A.J. ran over to him and hugged his waist. Without pause, he gave him a brief hug and kissed the top of his sleep-tousled locks.

"Good morning, buddy," Aiden answered, unaware of the sappy grin covering his face at the sight of his son.

"What are you cooking?" A.J. questioned going to sit at the table with his grandfather.

"Scrambled eggs, turkey sausages and whole wheat toast," Aiden informed happily.

"Mmm," A.J. licked his lips as he sat patiently waiting at the kitchen table.

"That does sound good," Mr. Kapahu said patting his belly hungrily. "I'm starving."

Kai agreed as she set the mug of coffee near the stove where he stood.

"I heard strenuous activity does that to you," Aiden smirked, eyes glowing mischievously.

Before he could move away, Kai pinched him playfully on the ass.

"Okay, you two," Mr. Kapahu admonished good-naturedly looking up from his paper. "There is a child present."

A.J. giggled bringing him back from his lustful thoughts.

"Food's ready," Aiden announced as he brought the filled dishes of hot food to the table. Everyone helped themselves, except A.J., who was served by him.

"Hmm," Kai hummed appreciatively. "It's delicious." Her father shook his head in agreement. "Did Bobby Flay teach you how to make this?" Kai tapped her lower lip playfully. "Or was it, Anne Burrell?"

Aiden's head bowed in mock shame.

"I'm never gonna live that down, am I?"

"Nope," she rebuked with a smug smile.

A.J. sat staring at him, a brow arched in thought.

"What's the matter, buddy?" Aiden studied his little boy.

"Mr. Kaplan?"

"Yes, A.J.?"

His son smiled at him, blue eyes as clear as the cloudless Hawaiian sky outside the kitchen window.

"When can I start calling you daddy?"

Stunned by the comment, Kai choked on her orange juice, sputtering and coughing into her napkin. Mr. Kapahu gently patted his obviously shocked daughter on the back until she was able to breathe normally again.

"A.J.," she responded as calmly as she could. "Who told you Mr. Kaplan is your father?"

Kai glanced at her father with a dagger-like stare, nostrils flaring in anger.

"No way," Joseph claimed, sounding as surprised as she did; his Hawaiian lilt strengthened under his livid daughter's scrutiny. "I didn't say *noth'in*."

She looked back at A.J.

"Who told you?" she asked again, her usually dormant Hawaiian accent stronger because of her stress.

"Nobody," the little boy shrugged.

"Are you telling me the truth?" she grilled. "Nennie didn't tell you?"

"Mommy," he sighed looking at her directly—blue eyes to amber eyes. "I figured it out on my own."

"How?" Aiden queried, wanting to know the details.

A.J. sighed again.

"I'm five…I'm in kindergarten…and I can read," he boldly explained.

"Okay," she grumbled. "What does that have to do with anything—"

"You have my birth certificate framed on your wall," he interrupted his mother's statement, his tone confident. "My daddy's name is written on it… *Aiden Joseph Kaplan*."

"Wow!" Aiden shook his head in disbelief.

"And…" his son continued, "…we have the same-colored eyes…and the same face…and the same chin…but we have different hair. My hair is black and wavy, and Mr. Kaplan's is dark brown and straight…and…I'm more tanned…*and*…"

"Okay, alright, I got it...I got it," she winced. "I'm an idiot."

Aiden cleared his throat.

"When did you know it was *me*?"

"At the beach last Sunday."

A.J. smiled a beautiful, innocent smile.

"I can't believe you figured this out all by yourself," Kai whispered.

"So?" A.J. turned back to his wide-eyed father. "May I call you daddy?"

Aiden stood, walked over to his genius of a son, and kissed him on the forehead, his heart swelling with pride inside his chest.

"I would love it if you called me daddy." His eyes were beginning to get misty. "I love you, son."

A.J. giggled then took a big bite of his toast. Aiden glanced at Kai, a steady stream of tears flowing down her silky, honey complexion. He winked at her and watched as the tension seemed to flow out of her too. Quickly he stood, kissed her on the cheek and went back to his breakfast, happy and content.

CHAPTER NINE

"Kai?" Aiden pounded on the bathroom door. "What's taking so long? I thought you only had to pee."

"Go away!" she yelled. "I'm busy."

It was turning out to be the longest two minutes of her life as she sat on the closed toilet lid, staring at the plastic stick, awaiting her fate.

"Did you fall in?" he teased.

She growled loudly.

"Do I bother you when you're in here?" she huffed.

"No, but wait…did you just growl at me?"

She shook her head in exasperation. The man could be such a…

Another knock vibrated the wooden barrier separating the bathroom from the outer hallway.

"Mommy," A.J. spoke next. "Are you sure you're okay?"

Great!

Instead of one little boy harassing her, Kai was surrounded by two, big Aiden and little Aiden. She was losing her mind.

"Could you please give me…" she glanced at her watch. "…a couple of minutes?"

The *big* pain-in-her-ass laughed loudly from behind the closed door, and then she heard the doorknob jiggle and silently thanked God she had remembered to lock it in her haste to take the pregnancy test she had snuck into the bathroom under her t-shirt.

"Are you sure you're alright?" Aiden's voice lowered with concern.

"Yes," she lied to the back of the door. "I'll be out in one more minute."

It had been almost three weeks since the "oops" moment in Aiden's kitchen. Lately, she'd been feeling tired and sometimes certain smells would make her nauseous. This morning, however, she actually threw up her breakfast. She'd played it off as if she had caught the stomach flu going around the hospital. Right on cue, her stomach lurched again, but she refused to give in to it, terrified that Aiden and A.J. would hear.

Kai glanced at her watch again. Time was up and she wasn't ready for the results. Steeling herself, she picked-up the stick.

One line…not pregnant, two lines…*Holy crap!*

Holy! Crap!

Kai paced the length of the bathroom. The cheerfully decorated space suddenly made her violent. She was pregnant. Again! By the pain-in-the-ass love of her life.

The North Shore was crowded with tourists and locals alike all out to enjoy a perfect day of surfing. It was a tropical seventy-eight degrees with a temperate ocean-scented breeze caressing the Hawaiian coastline and not a cloud in the sky. Kai knew some of the participants in the surf competition supporting the local children's hospital and wanted to introduce him to them, but Aiden was content to spend time with the woman of his dreams and their son. As far as he was concerned, life couldn't possibly get any better.

"Mommy, may I go see Pappy?"

"Go ahead, but don't run. You might fall," Kai yelled, right as A.J. took off at a gallop toward her parents' food truck.

Aiden could only laugh at the selective hearing of the energetic little boy.

"Don't worry. He's a typical boy. If he falls, he'll just get up and brush himself off. No worries."

"I'm the one who has to bandage him up if he does get hurt," she scoffed, giving him an angry glare.

He shook his head.

"No, I'm here now," he comforted. "I can bandage him up."

"I forgot, you're here for another eight weeks," she replied sarcastically under her breath.

Kai had been in a foul mood all day and he decided to let it go before she kept her earlier promise about castrating him. He wasn't sure what he had done to make her so angry, but he sure as hell didn't want to inadvertently do it again.

"Did I do something wrong?"

The look she gave him could have melted his face right off of his skull. That was his cue to shut up.

"Aloha, Pappy!" A.J. stood outside of his grandfather's colorfully decorated food truck.

Joseph stuck his head out and looked down, smiling when A.J. came into view.

"Aloha, kolohe," Mr. Kapahu laughed. "Are you here to see the surfing competition?"

"Sir, yes, sir," the boy answered as he saluted. "We're meeting Uncle Koa here. Uncle Marcus and Aunty Vanessa are coming too. They're going to watch the competition with us."

"Solid," Mr. Kapahu said, smiling at his favorite grandson, actually his only grandson.

Marcus had spent some time with the Kapahu's when Kai attended USC and more recently since Aiden, Kai and A.J. were becoming their own little family. Marcus and Vanessa had become honorary Kapahu's, joining the ranks of seemingly hundreds of biological and extended 'cousins.' They attended Sunday beach brunch/volleyball tournaments as well as joining them to see movies and going out to eat on different occasions. Kai and Vanessa had also become fast friends over the last couple of weeks and A.J. adored Marcus, always wanting to ask him questions about his soon-to-be-born baby.

"Where are your mom and dad?" Joseph questioned.

A.J. turned and pointed as the two adults came up the sidewalk holding hands. A soft laugh escaped his lips.

"*Aloha*, Papa," Kai greeted him in a less than enthusiastic manner.

"Are you ok?" her father frowned.

"Fine," she huffed, abruptly.

"Hmm," he replied his brow arching up.

"Where's Nennie?" A.J. jumped up and down, unsuccessfully trying to see into the food truck's high window.

"She went to Uncle Choy's bakery to pick-up more Hawaiian rolls for the sandwiches," the astute former mechanical engineer told. "She should be back any minute."

"Papa, could I get a ginger ale, please?" Kai requested, clutching her stomach, a sick expression on her sallow face.

"Sure."

Mr. Kapahu disappeared into the truck for a minute. He returned with Kai's ginger ale, two bottles of water, and several disposable containers of white rice, kimchi (a Korean-style of pickled vegetables), and mouth-watering golden-fried, jumbo shrimp. Aiden's stomach growled.

"Thanks Mr. Kapahu."

Aiden nodded as he took the items from his future father-in-law.

"Aiden, we're practically family, call me Joseph or Papa, okay?"

"Yes, sir...I mean yes...Joseph." He blushed.

It seemed natural calling Kai's father by his first name. Maybe after he and Kai got married he would call him Papa. Since he didn't have his own father in his life, he liked the idea of Joseph and Leilani as surrogate parents. After all, he'd known Kai's parents since he was nineteen and they had always treated him like a second son. He felt his chest tighten again.

Every birthday during his four years at USC, Mrs. Kapahu had sent him birthday cards and packages of macadamia nuts, dried Hawaiian fruits like pineapple and papaya, gourmet Kona coffee beans and t-shirts sporting their company's logo. At Thanksgiving and Christmas, Kai would bring back traditional Hawaiian holiday foods and sweets for him to indulge in, saying that her mother said, "You're too skinny and need to be fattened up."

Aiden smiled to himself as he led his small family to an empty picnic table a few feet away from the food truck.

"Here you go, son." He handed A.J. one of the containers of food and a bottled water.

"Thank you, Daddy."

The simple show of respect made him feel ten feet tall.

"You're welcome." Aiden gave Kai her food and soda. "Here you go. This one is yours."

"Mahalo." Kai opened the bottle and began taking small sips.

Aiden knew something was wrong when she allowed him to steal several of the mouth-watering shrimp off of her plate.

"You don't look so well." He leaned over to feel her forehead. "You feel a little clammy."

"My stomach isn't feeling well," she spoke in an emotionless tone.

"Would you like something other than ginger ale, some tea instead?"

"No." She shook her head, her voice almost too low to hear. "I have something to tell you."

He arched a brow, worry lines creasing his forehead.

"Ok," he grimaced. "Now I'm nervous."

Kai turned to A.J., who had just finished his last shrimp and was silently studying her plate.

"Mommy are you going to eat those?" he probed.

Kai smiled and put her disposable container with the remaining food in front of him. He grinned as he started working on the flavorful morsels.

Aiden frowned at her unusual behavior.

"Now I know you're sick."

Frowning back, she turned to A.J. and asked, "A.J., can you hang out with Uncle Koa for a few moments while Daddy and I talk?"

"Okeedokeeartichokee," he sang as he grabbed his container and bottled water.

In silence, they watched him join Koa near the water's edge, his uncle busy talking with a few Navy buddies. Koa scooped him up and put him on his shoulders. Their son sat contentedly on his perch nibbling on a rather large shrimp.

Cautiously, Aiden reached across the table and rested his hand over hers. He could feel them shaking, but he didn't comment on it.

"Tell me. Whatever it is, please," he pleaded. "Because right now you're scaring the tar out of me."

Overwhelmed with everything, she opened her mouth to speak, then closed it, then repeated the movement once again. Her motions reminding him of a fish out of water gasping for breath, he was afraid she might hyperventilate.

"I'm pregnant, Aiden," the words rushed out as she started to cry.

All the blood left his head. Thank goodness he was already sitting. Kai scrutinized his reaction from beneath a cascade of tears.

"Please don't cry." He pulled her against his side, trying to comfort her. "I know it's a shock, but it will all be okay. I promise."

"You did this to me, again," she sobbed uncontrollably. "I'm never having sex with you again."

"Whoa!" he blurted, his cock starting to panic. "Don't get carried away now. There's no reason to jump the gun."

"You self-absorbed bastard," she hissed, making him recoil. "Every time I have sex with you, I end up knocked-up."

"Wait a minute," he reminded, lowering his voice. "The first time we had sex I used a condom, remember? It's not my fault it broke."

"Fine, that was a fluke, but the morning at your apartment you just slipped it in without even thinking about the consequences."

She was hiccupping now, bringing curious gazes their way.

"Now I'm...*Damn*...don't touch me."

"I'm sorry. I'm so sorry, Kai."

He stroked her shoulders when she allowed him to hold her again.

"I'm going to take care of you and A.J. and everything will be fine. I promise. Everything will be fine."

On the verge of hysteria, Kai brushed away the remaining tears. The sight of her in this much pain made him feel ill, but he honestly believed with his whole being that everything would be alright.

"How will it be fine when you're leaving in a few months, Aiden?" she wept. "My life is here. Our son's life is here. If it wasn't for my family, I don't know what I would have done all those years ago."

"I know it was difficult—"

"You don't know what it was like, Aiden," she interjected. "I was pregnant and scared and thinking you not only abandoned me, but also our unborn child." She struggled to regain control of her emotions. "I hated you for a long time."

Her words were battering against his soul, breaking his heart knowing the agony he had unknowingly caused her...that his father had caused her.

Determined to comfort her, he pulled her into his lap even while she struggled.

"Kai, listen to me." He wiped her tears away with his thumbs. "I can't change the past. I wish I could. I can only do right by you going forward. Do you believe that if I had known about you and A.J., I would have come for you?"

Nervously, he held his breath waiting for the next emotional blow she would slam him with, but it never came.

"I believe you would have come for us," she whispered, her breathing beginning to return to normal.

"Good." He gently kissed her trembling lips. "I love you, Kai. Not because of the amazing sex," he paused, "although that's enough for me. I love you because you believe in me more than I believe in myself. I promise you it's going to all work out."

And he honestly believed it.

CHAPTER TEN

Aiden wanted everything to be perfect. He had spoken to Kai's Aunty Barbara, a highly sought-after caterer and classically trained chef, who was on her way to the marina to drop-off the food. With her help, he had carefully chosen the menu filled with all of Kai's favorite things to eat. The items would be delivered directly to the Honolulu Marina and Yacht Club, which gave him one less thing to worry about.

As luck would have it, he also found the perfect venue for the occasion. Joseph's brother, Daniel, owned a fleet of catamarans and yachts he chartered to high-end clientele that came with a captain, crew, and steward for a reasonable fee for the night. He had even managed to convince Uncle Daniel to allow him and Kai to spend the night on the luxury vessel without the crew. Reluctantly, the man agreed saying the crew could go back to shore after dinner using the emergency speedboats and come back the following afternoon.

Daniel also arranged to stock the boat with several bottles of Aiden's favorite champagne, breakfast items for the following morning, along with bouquets of native orange birds-of-paradise, plum, pink, and white calla lilies, and a variety of orchids from Leilani's sister, Marie the florist, who owned her own wholesale floral shop. Her cousin, Keanu, was providing one of his town cars for the evening, free of charge. All Aiden had to do was tip the driver. Nervous about the evening, Aiden kept reviewing his mental checklist afraid he might have forgotten something.

He even went as far as renting a classic black tux, James Bond style, and purchasing a gold evening gown for Kai he'd seen at a boutique while he and Vanessa were ring shopping. Vanessa agreed she would look stunning in it and he had no doubt about that. She could look irresistible in a burlap sack. The dress was a little pricey, $900 to be exact, but he figured Kai could wear it to special dinners and functions on base and when they moved back to Annapolis. Another subject he hadn't brought up with her. He dismissed the thought, deciding to cross that bridge when he came to it. He didn't want to ruin their night.

Hoping to calm his nerves, Aiden patted his pant pocket making sure he had the most important item of the night...the ring. He had enlisted Vanessa's help in choosing the perfect engagement ring. The two women were always talking about food and fashion, so he figured Vanessa would know what she would like. After visiting several local jewelry stores, Aiden found what he was looking for. A two-carat, flawless, Marquise-cut diamond solitaire with surrounding sapphire baguettes in a platinum setting.

He hoped she would know he chose the sapphires because that was the color his eyes turned when he thought of her...and all of the naughty things he wanted to do to her. He'd keep that last part to himself. It was a work of art. Handmade and one of a kind...just like her. It was perfect and he couldn't wait to slip it on her finger.

A.J. was spending the night with Marcus and Vanessa so they could have a romantic evening alone. Marcus said it would be good practice for them having a kid in the house. Vanessa could go into labor at any time, and he was actually glad for the company.

Checking to make sure the town car would be picking him up on time, he ran to the bedroom to get his cell phone and wallet. Since Kai was pregnant...again, he didn't have to wear condoms anymore. He smiled to himself. Yeah, she was right. He was a bastard, but he wanted tonight to be one Kai would never forget. He felt like a nervous wreck. After all, it wasn't every day you asked the woman of your dreams to marry you.

A knock on the front door announced Aiden's arrival. Kai took one last look at her reflection in the full-length mirror and inhaled deeply. The dress Aiden had sent over was an exquisite form-fitting, halter evening gown of burnished gold. The floor-length, raw silk gown brought out the gold specks in her eyes and enhanced the naturally golden hues of her skin. He even remembered a pair of matching strappy gold wedge sandals.

Her mom helped put her hair up into an elegant chignon allowing her to show off her neck, which she knew was one of Aiden's favorite places to kiss. She kept her make-up simple, a little gold eye shadow, eyeliner, and gold-tinted lip gloss. Kai smiled; confident he'd love how she looked.

Another annoyed knock could be heard…and he called her impatient.

Geez!

Feeling a bit flustered, she grabbed the gold evening bag she borrowed from Vanessa and practically jogged to the door, yanking it open before he could knock again.

"Good grief, what took you so long—" Aiden stumbled over the last part of his sentence as he examined her from head to toe then back again.

Obviously pleased, he released a long, low whistle.

"You look like a goddess."

Unwillingly, she blushed as he placed his hand at the small of her back, leading her to the awaiting car and uniformed driver who she recognized as one of her extended family members. The chauffeur gave them an appreciative smile before opening the door for them. Then waited as Aiden helped her into the back seat then climbed in beside her.

Inside the vehicle was all polished, dark wood and brushed-gold accents. There was a fully stocked bar with everything from aged brandy to sugar-free sodas and imported sparkling mineral water. There was even a TV and music system for their enjoyment.

"What are we celebrating?" she asked nervously.

"You'll see," was his only reply.

"Is there something going on at the Navy base?" she prodded.

"Nope."

Instantly, she was on high alert.

"Aiden, tell me what's happening."

"Can't you relax and enjoy the moment?" he chastised, relishing the upper

hand.

"I guess so." She nibbled on her bottom lip to keep her mind focused on the moment.

"You don't get sea-sick, do you?" Aiden inquired, holding his breath.

"No, not usually," she blurted as she studied him curiously. "Why?"

"You'll see."

He took her hand in his and squeezed gently.

The rest of the trip, they drove in silence appreciating the sultry jazz filling the town car's immaculate interior. The rich scent of leather with a hint of citrus calming her nervousness.

"You're being very secretive tonight," she accused, admiring his handsome profile.

"Am I?"

"Uh huh," she nodded.

Quietly he sat, his thumb tracing circles over the back of her hand he was holding.

"We haven't been a couple for very long, so I know I'm not forgetting an anniversary of some sort."

He smiled that same mischievous smile that warned of wickedly, delicious things to come.

"Aiden," she said sounding annoyed. "Tell me what's going on."

He chuckled smugly.

"It's a surprise."

"Tell me."

Aiden shook his head.

"Can't you be patient?"

"Scoundrel," she hissed playfully.

"Pain," he hissed back.

Unexpectedly, he leaned toward her stopping a hairsbreadth away from her lips. The unique scent of sandalwood and musk created havoc on her already overly sensitized libido. Her clit instinctively began to pulse, and she could feel her sex dampen.

Oh! No!

Not now!

Not in this amazingly expensive dress!

Swiftly, she sat straighter trying not to show any weakness toward him. Hoping desperately, he couldn't sense her arousal. If he did, she'd never make it out of the car un-ravished. The man was a brute.

He chuckled again, his eyes that familiar dark sapphire, almost glowing in the dim light of the car.

"Don't try to hide it." He kissed the side of her mouth sweetly. "I already know."

"Know, what?" she whispered, hoping the driver couldn't hear their conversation through the raised glass panel.

"That you're hot and wet for me," he accused. His voice thick and laced with lust. "I want to take you right here…right now…I don't even care if the driver hears us."

"Damn it," she moaned when his lips finally descended on her. "No, Aiden, please don't. I know him…he's practically family."

She spoke against his soft, full lips. Kai had no doubt if he wanted to he could get her to agree to almost anything. Including having sex in the back seat of the rental car.

Aiden pulled away, still grasping her slender hand in his much larger ones, and sat back in the seat, eyes closed, but his cheeks were slightly flushed.

"Don't worry," he soothed then waggled his brows in an arrogant manner. "I'm going to save the good stuff for later."

As she was about to give her saucy retort, the car pulled into the Honolulu Marina and Yacht Club forty minutes later and parked in front of a skit with the most luxurious fifty-foot yacht they had ever seen. The boat's white hull gleamed under the full Hawaiian moon.

"What...*how*...Aiden, how did you do this?"

"It seems if you're a member of the Kapahu clan, which now I am, the world is your oyster," he divulged with a grin.

She smiled knowingly, leaning close to his ear as she whispered, "This is one of my Uncle Daniel's boats, isn't it?"

Aiden nodded. "He gave me a great deal for the boat and the crew for the night," he informed, smiling proudly.

"For the night?"

A frown marred her otherwise flawless features.

"Yup," he answered. "Marcus and Vanessa agreed to watch our little *kolohe* tonight. So, we can relax and enjoy."

Quickly, he tipped the driver, then took her hand and led her up the walkway to the yacht. They were immediately greeted by their steward, a young man in his mid-twenties with blonde hair and green eyes, who kept ogling his soon to be fiancé. The other man obviously appreciated Kai's exotic beauty. He couldn't fault him for that, but he did inform their steward to back the hell off with a very blatant stare. Filled with embarrassment, the steward's cheeks reddened at the look he gave him.

"*Aloha*, Mr. Kaplan...Miss Kapahu. My name is Justin, and I will be taking care of you this evening. Please, follow me."

Justin led them to the lower deck of the ship to a small, but elegantly decorated dining room.

"Wow!" Kai exclaimed under her breath, and he had to agree.

The yacht, appropriately named *The Hawaiian Goddess*, was a ship builder's dream come true, with dark cedar walls and floors, and white and cream accents with pops of aquamarine to soften the masculine space. Above the glass and brass dining table was a small antique chandelier that mimicked the materials of the table below it. Throughout the cabin were several handmade Oriental rugs in varying shades of cream, green, gold, and aquamarine. It was overwhelming and hopefully unforgettable.

Attentively, Aiden pulled out Kai's chair and waited for her to be seated, then walked around to his seat located directly across from her. She looked stunning. Amber eyes appearing even more golden, soft skin glowing under the lighting of the chandelier, hair pulled up allowing him to admire her slender neck. Simple diamond studs adorned her lick-able earlobes sparkling every time she turned her head. The look she graced him with was filled with so much tenderness, love, and desire his heart hurt and he couldn't help reaching out for her hand again. She rested her other hand over his. The simple touch warmed his entire body.

"This is magnificent," Kai whispered as she glanced around the dining room.

"You're magnificent," his voice came out hoarse.

Soon after, Justin returned to fill their goblets with water and uncorked the Champagne. Filling their *Swarovski* crystal Champagne flutes with chilled 2002 *Dom Perignon Vintage Rose*. Aiden couldn't help but laugh when Kai's eyebrows arched almost completely up to her hairline.

The other man returned the bottle of Champagne to the silver ice bucket before rushing off once again. Returning promptly with a tray containing an assortment of chilled jumbo shrimp with cocktail sauce, mushrooms stuffed with crab, and bacon and chive mini-quiche. Justin left the tray in the middle of the table for them to help themselves and hurried back to the galley to prepare the rest of their gourmet dinner.

"Are you allowed to drink alcohol while you're pregnant?" he wondered out loud.

Kai giggled, knowing he felt out of his element about the entire pregnancy process.

"One glass is allowed."

They both reached for their Champagne flutes at the same time, taking a tentative sip.

"Mmm," Kai sighed. "I've never cared for Champagne, but I think you may have converted me."

Her smile illuminated the room.

Aiden laughed.

"I knew you'd like it."

"Did you get a promotion I don't know about?" Kai teased, taking another sip.

"Like I said, your family has a lot of clout on the island," he replied sheepishly. "Plus, I've been alone for so long, I have a nice nest egg set aside. Believe me I can afford it."

"Whatever you say, Lieutenant Kaplan," she beamed, and the worry lines softened.

More at ease, they made small talk while sampling the scrumptious appetizers.

"The stuffed mushrooms are delicious," she cooed, reaching for another one. A low moan escaped her lips, causing his cock to harden.

Good grief!

Not now!

Not until we're alone!

He silently chastised his lower appendage. She moaned again when he fed her a large succulent shrimp.

"Don't do that, Kai," he whispered while staring at her mouth.

"Do what?" she queried, confusion filling her eyes.

"Moan like that," he said dryly.

"I didn't moan," she adamantly denied.

"Yes, you did moan," he chuckled at her offended tone.

"Ok," she said still confused. "Why can't I moan?"

Aiden gulped loudly.

"Because you make that same sound when we're making love."

Kai tried unsuccessfully to stifle her laughter.

"So?"

"So," he whispered. "Unless you want me to clear this table and fuck you until we both can't walk…in front of Justin…then I suggest you behave."

He ended his chastisement with a wink.

His words must not have sat well with Kai because an impish gleam suddenly appeared in her eyes, and he knew he was in trouble.

Slowly, she reached for the tray, took another shrimp and dipped it gingerly into the cocktail sauce, careful to get only a little of the spicy red sauce. Holding it by the tail she slowly raised it to her lips. Her eyes closing as it disappeared into her mouth, her pink tongue darting out to lick a bit of sauce that was at the corner of her mouth. Aiden's balls immediately drew up and his member was so hard it could hammer nails. Now in agony, he shifted uncomfortably on his seat.

"Mmm," she moaned softly, eyes lowering.

"Kai, I'm warning you," he snickered at her playfulness.

"Uh hum," Justin cleared his throat before entering the room, cheeks flushed.

Aiden wondered how much of their conversation he had overheard and felt a little guilty at the man's discomfort. Kai, on the other hand, had an arrogant smirk on her face, which made him want to spank her.

Maybe later.

Focused on his task, Justin removed the appetizer tray from the table resting it on a nearby rolling cart. Close, but out of the way. He refilled their beverages then retrieved their dinners, placing the dishes in front of them with practiced grace. Then with a flourish he simultaneously lifted the silver domed lids covering the gold-accented Wedgewood China.

Kai's eyes widened to the size of saucers and Aiden knew he had remembered correctly. The plates in front of them had Beef Wellington with a classic burgundy sauce, steamed broccoli and lobster-twice-baked potatoes. Her face lit up like a child on Christmas morning getting ready to tear into its presents. His girl did love to eat.

"Bon appetite!" Their steward smiled at the appreciative glances. "I'll be back to check on you shortly."

As soon as he disappeared into the hallway, they both dug in. Aunt Barbara really outdid herself. The Beef Wellington was nicely seasoned and melted in your mouth. The broccoli was still a bit crunchy, which was how Kai liked it, and the delicate chunks of lobster in the potatoes made *him* want to moan.

"I can't believe you remembered all of my favorite dishes," she stated, practically glowing.

"I've told you before…I never forgot about you," his voice cracked revealing his emotion and love for her.

She grinned.

"You can be such a charmer when you want to be."

"Would you please excuse me?" Aiden stood and made his way to the hallway leading to the galley. "I'll be right back."

He returned a few moments later and finished his dinner while chatting with Kai. It always amazed him they could talk about anything, from politics to ice skating to the current situation in the Middle East. It had been this way since they had first met. He was such an idiot for not marrying her after they had graduated college, but he would soon rectify that.

When the dinner dishes were cleared, and the dessert was laid in front of them covered with smaller silver lids, Justin smiled knowingly, and Aiden felt as if he'd throw up, but instead he simply observed Kai.

Finally, the lids of the desserts were removed with another one of Justin's dramatic flourishes revealing a decadent chocolate soufflé dusted with powdered sugar and garnished with a fresh mint leaf on his plate and a small black velvet box on Kai's. It took her a moment to comprehend. In the meanwhile, their steward had already disappeared from the room, leaving them alone. Stunned, Kai stared at the box while Aiden stared at her.

"Open it," he commanded anxiously.

She did what she was told, hands shaking slightly as she picked-up the box.

"Aiden?"

"Open the box," he urged with excitement.

At last, she flipped open the tiny lid revealing the diamond and sapphire ring inside. Aiden heard her breath hitch, followed by a muffled sob.

"Aiden," she gasped, voice low and breathless. "It's impeccable."

Reaching over, he took the ring out of her hand and came around the table, dropping to one knee in front of her.

"Ali'ikai Leilani Kapahu, you have been my best friend…my advocate…the mother of my child and the woman of my dreams for as long as I can remember. Please, do me the honor of becoming my wife."

He took a deep breath feeling the emotions filling his chest.

"Will you marry me: *Amazon*?" He grinned roguishly.

"I would love to marry you: *Beast*."

Kai wanted to pinch herself to make sure it wasn't a dream.

"Did you pick this out all by yourself?" she beamed.

"Vanessa helped," Aiden admitted bashfully.

"It's beautiful." She wiggled her fingers admiring the way the jewels sparkled under the light. "It must have cost a small fortune."

"It was worth it." He kissed her chastely. "You're worth it."

Thank heaven she had liked it, loved it, actually. From the moment he placed the exquisite bauble on her ring finger, she couldn't take her eyes off of it. He couldn't either. With every movement of her hand, the flawless diamond caught the light, refracting the beams like tiny rainbows. The sparkle of the dark sapphires accented it even more.

"You're such a pig though."

"Why am I a pig?" he grinned. "Look around you. I'm freaking awesome."

"Wow!" Kai snorted. "If your head gets any bigger you'll sink the boat."

He laughed loudly, pulling her closer to him as they snuggled on the sofa.

"Why am I a pig?" he repeated.

"Only you would be so brazenly sexual as to put sapphires on my engagement ring."

He stared at her with mock indignation.

"I don't know what you're referring to."

"My ass!" she chuckled. "Your eyes turn this color blue, whenever you want some…you know."

"Whenever I want some…*what*?"

"You know *what*."

"Say it." He laughed again enjoying her discomfort. "I dare you to say it."

"Sex," she mumbled, covering her eyes like a toddler playing hide-n-seek. "There... happy?"

"I'll show you what'll make me happy." He pulled her on top of him, their chests pressed together. "I love you."

"I love you too."

With her index finger, she traced a line across his lips, giggling when his tongue darted out to taste her.

"Mmm, you taste like chocolate, and Champagne, and deliciously sinful things," he growled.

"You got that with one lick?" she blushed.

"I'm talented like that."

"Mahalo for tonight. It couldn't have been more wonderful." She brought her hand up and lightly touched his cheek with her knuckles, enjoying the tiny stubbles beginning to grace his tanned face.

"You're more than welcome," he replied, slowly lowering his lips to hers.

Kai avoided his lips and instead kissed the tip of his nose enjoying his ability to just *be*.

"I don't want a long engagement," Aiden stated suddenly. "I want to get you *balled-and-chained* to me as soon as possible."

She rolled her eyes.

"Well." She thought for a moment before saying, "What about in three months? That should be enough time to set a date, find a venue, order the invitations—"

"No, that's too long," he began. "How about in two weeks?"

Her mouth fell open at his request. How could she arrange a large wedding in such a short period of time? Regardless of her family's clout as Aiden liked to call it. Honestly, she couldn't see it coming together so soon.

"Aiden, I don't know if I can pull a wedding together in such a short time frame."

"Sure, we can," he assured. "Your family—"

"Our family," she stated firmly.

He grinned.

"Correction... *our family*... has the hook-up for everything, caterers, limos and town cars, luxury boats, wholesale flowers, everything we'll need. If you want, I'll take care of the arrangements myself," he smirked, knowing she'd never agree.

"No, that's okay," she informed, knowing that he knew she'd never let him handle something so important. "I'll figure it out."

"Kai, I don't want you stressed." He placed his hand over her tummy, rubbing gently. "It's not good for you or our daughter."

"How do you know it's a daughter?" she giggled. "It could be another son."

"A son would be excellent too," he agreed. "But I like the idea of a little girl with curly, dark hair and almond-shaped amber eyes."

Kai giggled at his sincere declaration.

"Then you'll have to buy a gun to keep all of those no-good boys away."

"Damned right!" he grunted.

Wrapping her arms around his neck, she pulled him down to capture his lips. Using the tip of her tongue, she traced his bottom lip and felt the tremor that caused him to open his mouth on a gasp, allowing her invasion. She took the lead deepening the kiss, her tongue lashing out to duel with his. A slave to her ministrations, he groaned into her mouth creating a heady vibration that followed her spine all the way to her lower regions. Instantly, she was wet.

In tune to her needs, Aiden stroked her exposed back like she was a cat. Instinctively, she bowed against his firmly-packed body into the sensuous touch. Without permission, she reached between their bodies and quickly un-tucked his shirt, tunneling beneath the material to feel his chiseled abdomen. If her washing machine ever broke, she could always use his stomach.

"You feel incredible," Kai purred as she felt his growing erection against her pelvic bone.

"I feel even better without any clothes," he tried to convince the wily minx, daring her to undress him.

"I'd have to agree."

Eagerly, she kissed his neck, inhaling deeply to capture his fragrance.

"I need you, Kai," he moaned into her hair. "But not here."

Somehow Aiden managed to carry her to the cabin. The small space was decorated in creams, aquamarine, and chocolate brown. The king-sized bed took up most of the room, along with a six-drawer dresser, two night stands and a forty-two inch plasma television. Several porthole windows allowed slivers of moonlight into the area creating a dreamlike scene.

Carefully, he set her down near the bed, looking like the poster boy for sex, awaiting her instructions. She didn't know what to do.

"Aiden, I don't know what to do."

Aiden cupped her cheek with his palm, and she turned into it loving its warmth.

"This is your night, baby," he spoke in a hushed tone. "Do with me what you wish."

The few times they had made love, Aiden had always taken the lead. It never occurred to her she should be the instigator, but he stood in front of her looking all innocent and trusting and all she wanted to do was…devour him…every freaking, hard inch of him.

"Take off your shoes and socks," she whispered feeling a bit nervous about being in control.

Surprisingly, he did as he was told, removing the items as she followed his movements enjoying the flexing of his toned biceps and the rippling of his well-used back muscles beneath his shirt. Unable to resist any longer, she reached up, removed his bowtie and undid his top button. Placing small kisses on his chest as the smooth, tanned flesh appeared in her wake. Her mouth went dry. When all of the buttons were undone, she slowly pushed his shirt away from his shoulders and watched as it fell to the floor behind him.

"Take these off too." She tugged on his belt and waistband.

At her command, he quickly unbuckled and unzipped his pants allowing them to fall to the floor before stepping out of them, standing in front of her wearing only his black boxer briefs. Kai couldn't help licking her lips. The image of her handsome fiancé standing in front of her like *Michelangelo's David* was overwhelming and she debated whether she should relinquish her control or lack thereof, back to Aiden.

He must have sensed her hesitation.

"You can do it, baby," he urged. "I know how much you enjoy bossing me around."

Naturally, his words spurred her into action. Which she knew was his intention.

"Lay in the middle of the bed," she ordered with more confidence.

Kai waited patiently until Aiden was lying in the middle of the bed propped up on a bunch of pillows before she slowly began to undress. First, she reached behind her back to unzip her dress allowing it to fall gently to the floor before stepping out of it and putting it on a small wooden valet at the foot of the bed. His eyes widened and he swallowed hard.

"Fuck! Me!" he muttered under his breath. His chest rising and falling like he had just run a marathon.

She smiled wickedly.

"I fully intend to do just that," she stated with her newly found confidence.

Next, she reached around and unhooked her strapless bra allowing it to land at her feet. She kept her black silk thong on, giving him something to remove.

With all of the grace she could muster, she crawled onto the bed, hoping she looked as sexy as she felt. She must have been doing it right because she heard him say something like, "I'm gonna come before I even get into you," or something similar. Those words made her feel even more confident to complete her mission.

Giving her first blow-job.

Determination fueled her movements as she tucked her fingers into the waistband of his boxer briefs and slowly inched them down his powerful legs. She'd have to remember to write a letter thanking *Uncle Sam* for making sure her future husband stayed so damned fine.

When they were completely off, Kai glanced up and realized she was eye level with a very large, very thick, very angry-looking cock. It was humongous, with a bit of pre-cum on the wide, mushroom-shaped head. She gulped wondering how in the world something that size could fit inside her. Thank goodness she hadn't gotten a good look at it before because she might have stayed a virgin.

"Holy cow!" she whimpered.

Through the cloud of desire surrounding her, she heard Aiden chuckle at her muttered words.

"It's all for you, Kai."

Impatiently, he took his cock in hand and stroked his hard length from root to tip, making it grow even more.

"Stop doing that or it'll never fit," she tried to be flippant, but the shakiness in her voice revealed her anxiety. He stopped the motion of his hand and watched her lick her lips, desire and need filled her dripping sex.

With determination, she reached out, boldly taking his rock-hard flesh in both hands, holding him firmly like she'd seen him do. He felt like steel encased in satin. Kai stroked his shaft from root to tip fascinated by each rigid vein. Gently, she teased his balls almost giggling at the differences in texture of his cock. Leaning down she made an exploratory lick with her tongue. She felt powerful when she heard his breath hitch followed by the flex of his rod. Another tiny drop of pre-cum escaped the small slit at the tip and Kai wondered what it tasted like. Curiously, she moved toward the glistening liquid.

"Not everyone likes the taste of it," Aiden's lust-tinged voice warned.

Ignoring his statement, Kai licked it off with a lingering swipe of her tongue.

"Mmm," she moaned against the tip.

"Fuck!" he groaned through clenched teeth. "You're killing me. Take it in your mouth. Get it nice and wet so I can put it in your pussy."

Kai moaned as his explicit words made her clit throb, warmth filled her limbs and liquid desire filled her sex. Without hesitation, she engulfed the head of his cock with her mouth, using her tongue to trace invisible circles over the smooth head. Removing her mouth, she began pumping the thick base while running her tongue and lips over the stiff shaft.

"You taste sinful," she hummed against the monstrous flesh.

"Stop playing around," he pleaded. His words were strained, almost unrecognizable to her ears.

"Beg me," she ordered. "Beg me to suck your cock."

"Are you kidding?"

"Nope." She grinned wickedly. "I want you to beg to feel my lips giving you pleasure."

"C'mon…you can't be serious," her fiancé scoffed.

"Beg for it," she insisted.

"Please," he replied, rolling his eyes.

"Please, what?" She gently nipped the tip. Her boldness growing with every moan and rapid breath he took. "Beg me, damn it!"

Wow! She was really getting into this dominance thing.

"I've created a monster," Aiden admitted with a low chuckle. "Please, Kai... baby... love of my life... suck my fucking cock."

"Much better." She grinned before pulling his member back into her mouth.

Enthusiastically, she worked her lips and tongue up and down his shaft enjoying the feel. She only dared take half of it into her mouth, afraid she might gag and embarrass herself. All the while using her hands to pump the base. Several good strokes were all it took before Aiden stiffened and bucked a couple of inches off the bed.

"I'm gonna come," Aiden gasped. "If you don't want to swallow you better move."

But she did want to swallow. She wanted to taste every last wonderful inch of him. She wanted him to mark her as his. "Come for me, Aiden," she commanded, like he had often done to her.

And he did. Kai felt the thick jets of cum flooding her mouth as she drank every last drop.

"Holy! Shit!" he mumbled, pulling her up to kiss her lips while stroking her smooth back.

"How was I?" she blushed, holding her breath hoping her actions were pleasurable, or at least acceptable.

"I knew you'd be good at that, but damn girl. You're an expert." He looked at her curiously. "Are you sure you haven't done *that* to anyone before?"

She giggled and rolled her eyes.

"You are not the only one with natural skills," she jested playfully.

"I guess not."

Aiden couldn't believe his shy little Kai would be so aggressive in bed. The way she took control of him and sucked him to the most powerful orgasm he had ever experienced intrigued and overwhelmed him.

"Are you up for some more?" Kai lay on top of him, chest crushed against his, softly caressing his pecs. "Or do you need some time to recover?"

"You are *definitely* trying to kill me, aren't you?" he hissed, when she pinched his nipple then soothed the sting with her tongue. "What are you doing to me?"

"I don't know what you mean," she feigned innocence. "I was a helpless little lamb before I met you."

"Ha!" he protested. "Helpless my ass!"

Her eyes widened.

"I was innocent. Then the big, bad wolf…that's you…devoured me whole and ruined me for other men."

"I did, did I?" He nibbled, sucked, and licked the sweet flesh of her neck.

"Yup," she sighed, arching her neck to give him better access.

"I ruined you, huh?" his voice a sexy rasp.

"Uh huh," she gasped as he grabbed her ass and fondled the round, firm globes roughly.

"Well, then." He felt his cock stiffening to an almost painful point. "Then let me *ruin* you again," he informed while removing her thong.

Unrushed, he pumped his hips upward between her folds as Kai straddled him, amazed at the warm cream escaping her core. Taking his cue, Kai rose up on her knees to gain the height she needed, reached back for his cock and placed it directly at the entrance of her slick, wet folds. She whimpered as the tip pressed against the opening to her sex.

Pulling her down again, he held her tight.

"You're so damn wet, baby," he moaned against her neck. "It's so unbelievably hot."

"Mmm," she agreed pushing against him to take him deeper. His entire body stiffened when a pained yelp escaped her.

"What's wrong? Did I hurt you?" he asked, concern filling his voice.

"I can't." She wiggled her hips trying to take him inside. "It won't go in," her words tinged with frustration.

"Here," he stated, reaching between their bodies finding the tiny nubbin between her legs, "let me help you."

Using his thumb, he rubbed the slippery object in gentle circles. When Kai moaned and a rush of cream caressed his cock he pushed a little further inside. Before she could protest he found the nipple closest to him and began sucking and nipping at the stiff, dark peak.

"Aiden," her voice was a breathless wail as she worked his length into her extremely tight channel.

With one last firm thrust, he was lodged deep inside. He felt her inner muscles squeezing and sucking his hard-as-nails member and he prayed for enough control to give her the orgasm she desperately deserved. He withdrew his cock until only the head was still inside of her then reentered her wet heat on a slow glide. In and out. In and out. Feeling the tightening and clenching of her channel.

"Give it to me, baby," he urged. "Don't stop now."

Sitting up, Kai placed her hands on his chest for leverage and began a slow up and down rhythm on his shaft.

"That's it… just like that."

He grabbed lush, rounded hips and pumped her up and down at the same steady pace she had started. He felt her inner walls begin to tremor and he knew it wouldn't be much longer before she reached her climax. Her pace increased as she set a mind-blowing pace, up, down, up, down, until he almost saw stars.

"I'm close," she shouted, eyes closing on a breathy moan.

"Your pussy is like magic," he whispered.

"Aiden!" His name escaped her in a rush, making his cock swell even more. He'd burst soon. He was sure of it, for someone with hardly any sexual experience; the alluring female was a quick study. Hell…she was practically a professor.

Aiden increased his strokes working their bodies into a frenzied motion of sweaty limbs and pounding sex. They slammed against each other, pelvis to pelvis, finding that perfect rhythm.

"I can't last much longer." He forced himself to hold back the orgasm that was barreling down on him. He knew he was almost there when he felt his balls draw-up tight. Reaching behind her, he rubbed a finger in the overflowing cream coating the base of his cock then followed the seam of her ass to her puckered entrance. Gently, he began to stroke and tease her back entrance enjoying the sounds of pleasure escaping as she rode him to completion.

"That feels so good… don't stop… almost… almost there," she keened.

Aiden rubbed her rosette a bit harder.

"One day soon…I'm gonna take you…*here*," he promised. "I'm gonna fuck your ass so good you'll never want me to stop." He smacked her ass hard. "Would you like that you bad, bad girl?"

She didn't answer.

He smacked her again.

"Answer me, Kai. Do you want my cock in your ass?"

"Yes, Aiden… fuck, yes!" That was all the added stimulation his Hawaiian goddess needed to push her over the edge. Kai came with a rush of cream and an almost-painful cry. The strong spasms of her inner walls pulled the seed right out of him.

"Oh… my… *God!*" he yelled. Thankfully, they were out in the marina instead of at his apartment or, God forbid, her parents' house.

The force of his orgasm almost blinded him, his toes curled, his jaw clenched tight. He squeezed her ass so hard he felt her stiffen and he was certain he'd made a bruise. For several moments they lay there, Kai still on top of his chest, catching their breath and caressing each other with slow, easy strokes.

"Wow!" Aiden kissed her temple. "I've never been taken advantage of before," he teased. "A man could get used to it."

She giggled.

"Make sure I'm the only one who has that honor."

"I fully intend to," he smiled sincerely. "I was serious you know."

Kai's brows rose.

"Serious about what?"

He tapped a finger on her ass mischievously.

"Claiming your ass." He waggled his brows.

"We'll see." She smiled and closed her eyes.

"What does 'we'll see' mean?"

She smirked.

"You can claim mine… when I can claim yours."

With those words, Aiden drifted off to sleep wondering how he was ever going to keep up with her newfound sexual appetite. He had truly created a monster. He was a lucky, lucky man.

CHAPTER ELEVEN

Two weeks had flown by, and it was finally her wedding day. Kai waited nervously as her mom and aunts applied her make-up, styled her hair, and fussed over her like she was a princess in a fairytale. No matter how hard she had tried, she still couldn't believe today she would be marrying her best friend. She had dreamt of this moment, fantasized about it, but never had she believed it would actually happen.

"Done." Her mom smiled at her lovingly. "Turn around and take a look."

Slowly, she turned on the padded stool to look at her reflection in the vanity mirror. "Wow!"

She blinked back the tears threatening to overflow.

"Mama, I look like…*a bride*," she gasped, turning her head from side to side to see what her mother had done.

She had to admit, she looked better than expected considering she only slept three hours the night before. Was now having morning, afternoon, and evening sickness, and couldn't stop thinking about her fiancé, soon to be husband.

"Do you like it?" Leilani hoped.

"I love it, Mama!"

Leilani had swept her curls to the side, allowing the loose spirals to cascade over her shoulder. Then secured it with the same rhinestone-studded hair comb her mother had worn on her wedding day. Finally, she secured the traditional *haku*, a crown of white flowers, on her head. Since it was a morning wedding, Kai decided to go very natural with her make-up, eyeliner, mascara, and a neutral tinted lip gloss. She used a shimmering body lotion to give her skin a slight sparkle and her look was complete.

Well, almost complete.

"Time for the dress."

Her mom took her hand and led her to the middle of the bedroom. Anxiously, holding her breath as Aunty Marie unzipped the garment bag and brought her the stunning white, designer wedding gown specifically created for her by her cousin, Noelani. The young fashion designer had recently graduated from the *Fashion Institute of America* and wanted to take pictures of her wearing the dress to include in her design portfolio.

Needless to say, the one-of-a-kind dress was stunning. It was a simple sleeveless, white chiffon, A-line gown with hand-made flowers at the neckline and under the bodice, with a high-low hemline and a sweetheart neckline with dual straps for extra support to her bust line. For her footwear, she chose two-inch, white wedge sandals tastefully decorated with rhinestones on the straps, ideal for a beach wedding.

Her gorgeous wedding bouquet, created by Marie, the same aunt who was now helping her into her gown, had dark purple, pink, and white calla lilies. Just like the ones Aiden had used to decorate the yacht on the night he proposed. Her bridesmaids had similar bouquets as hers, but in all white.

She still couldn't believe she and her mom were able to pull together a wedding in only two weeks, but as Aiden always reminded; her family had the hook-up on everything. She had always wanted a beach wedding, so they didn't have to worry about booking a church or hall. Aunty Barbara provided her restaurant, which was usually closed on Sundays, which was the perfect reception facility. They only had to pay for the food and alcohol. To keep things simple, they made it a buffet so only the minimal wait staff was needed.

Her cousin, Jason, would DJ the reception. Uncle Ken, a professional mixologist, would handle the bar. Ken even surprised them with a specialty cocktail for the event called the *Kaiden* made with pineapple, mango, and papaya juice, vodka, and a splash of ginger ale. The creative mixologist even made a non-alcoholic version for her, Vanessa, and the children. Kai wished she could drink the alcohol version of the cocktail, but she still appreciated the thought.

"The limo is here," her father informed from the other side of the closed door.

When she opened the door, his jaw dropped.

"Ali'ikai," he choked back a sob. "You look…you look… you take my breath away."

"Don't make me cry, Papa." She hugged his neck tightly. "It'll ruin my make-up."

"Ok, you two." Leilani gently pried them apart while dabbing the corners of her eyes with a linen handkerchief. "You don't wanna be late for your own wedding."

Aiden hadn't had much sleep. Probably, two hours max, anxiety filling his mind. A.J. on the other hand had slept like a log, snoring softly like his mother. The two Kaplan men, along with Koa stayed at Marcus's temporary quarters on base since it was larger than his apartment. Which worked out well since Marcus was his best man and in charge of the bachelor party. Koa, his brother-in-law after today, had quickly bonded with both he and his friend. Even though Koa was just as annoying as his sister, they all had similar interests and goals. It also helped they were all in the Navy.

The quartet had gone to a local seafood festival on the North Shore instead of having a traditional bachelor party since he wanted to include A.J. in their merriment. They had gorged themselves on funnel cakes, fried seafood of every kind and frozen coconut custard. He was still full. They decided on cereal for breakfast knowing they were going to have a brunch reception.

Two weeks had passed in the blink of an eye with Kai taking care of every detail, except for her wedding band. Aiden chose a plain platinum band with three small sapphires decorating the top which she could wear with her engagement ring or alone when she went back to work. If she went back to work, after their weekend honeymoon with A.J. in Maui. He had rented a quaint cottage located on a private beach with nearby hiking trails and water sports activities he was certain his bride and son would love.

"Are you ready?" Marcus slapped him on the back.

"As I'll ever be," he said as he grinned and rubbed his hands together. "Can't wait for the honeymoon."

"Is that all you can think about?" Marcus chuckled.

"Yeah," he growled. "You know she made me abstain for the past two weeks, right?"

Marcus shook his head.

"She wants your first night as husband and wife to be special, memorable."

"You sound more like Vanessa every day," Aiden teased. "It wouldn't surprise me if you grew a vagina."

"Jack-off!" Marcus punched him in the arm.

"Dickhead!" Aiden punched back.

"Boys…boys." Vanessa slapped them both on the hands. "It's time to get going. We can't be late."

At exactly the right time, Kai heard the conch shell or *Pu*, (calling the earth, air, fire, and sea as witnesses) blown and knew it was time to start.

"Are you ready, baby girl?" Her father questioned as he guided her down the short path to the wedding pavilion.

"I've been ready for almost ten years," she replied with a bright smile.

The sight before them made her gasp and her father tightened his grip. White folding chairs were on each side of the aisle with a special white fabric runner, made specifically for beach weddings, sprinkled with purple and white orchid petals separating the groom's side from the bride's sides, even though everyone in attendance was related to her. She felt a sudden sadness for Aiden, whose father hadn't bothered to come even though she had sent him an invitation.

Pushing the thought out of her head, she focused instead on the small white pavilion on a raised platform. Standing there was the man of her dreams dressed in his service dress whites and looking much too debonair for his own good.

He stole her senses.

Beside him was Marcus, also in his whites, dark skin gleaming under the slowly rising Oahu sun. In front of them stood A.J., smiling and playing with the silk ring-bearers pillow. Koa was next to Marcus, dressed similarly and resembling *"The Rock"* even more than usual.

Her bridesmaids were equally stunning wearing plum chiffon knee-length dresses and matching plum sandals decorated with a few rhinestones on the strap. Each wearing their hair up in a casual chignon. They all smiled simultaneously at her except for Aiden, who mouthed, *"You look beautiful."*

Their gazes locked and she swore she saw him rub his hand over his heart muttering something and nudging Marcus discreetly with his elbow. The pounding in her chest suddenly flooded her ears as she walked toward her future. When she finally reached him, Joseph and Leilani put the traditional leis on both of their necks, a *ti* leaf lei around Aiden's neck and a white ginger lei around hers. They in turn did the same to her parents as was the ancient custom. Then the ceremony began.

Kai felt the air rush out of her lungs as her groom took her hand in his. Everything seemed to be moving in slow motion. Her eyes welled-up, her dark curls ruffling softly in the early-morning breeze and the man who had captured her heart all those years ago was going to be her husband.

Mine.

The *kahu*, or Hawaiian holy man, performed a customary Polynesian chant and with the song *Waiting for Thee* playing softly on the ukulele in the background they began their vow recital.

"Kai." Aiden looked at her, blue eyes to amber. "Never in my wildest dreams did I ever think you'd agree to marry me. You are the most intelligent...most beautiful...and the most difficult person I've ever known, and I wouldn't have you any other way. You are my heart and soul and lifeline, and I promise to love, honor, and cherish you for the rest of our lives."

Aiden gently squeezed her hands and she had to slowly inhale and exhale to compose herself.

Clearing her throat, she began.

"Aiden," she smiled up into those gray-blue irises and felt her heart lurch inside her chest. "The first time I saw you I wanted to kill you. The second time I saw you I wanted to be your friend. The third time I saw you I just wanted you, only you...always you. Today I accept all of you. The sexy, playful, intelligent, insufferable man I love. You are my heart and soul and lifeline, and I promise to love, honor, and cherish you for the rest our days."

As soon as she finished her vows, Marcus reached down, untied her ring from A.J.'s silk pillow and gave it to Aiden, who handed it to the holy man.

Kai turned to Vanessa, who was standing-in as her matron of honor looking beautiful, but extremely pregnant, and traded her bridal bouquet for the elegant platinum wedding band decorated with five small amber stones. She heard Aiden laugh at the fact they each chose similarly styled bands without knowing.

Continuing the ceremony, the *kahu* took both rings, dipped a *ti* leaf into a small bowl of sea water and sprinkled both rings with the water three times while he chanted in Hawaiian. While the priest completed his blessing over the bands, the flower girl placed colorful tropical flowers in a circle around her and Aiden. Next, they both poured two different colored sand into a container, symbolizing their unbreakable bond.

She grinned when Aiden mouthed, "How many traditions are there?"

"Don't be difficult," she mouthed back.

Finally, a lava rock was wrapped in a *ti* leaf and placed on the sand behind the pavilion to commemorate their union.

"Aiden," the *kahu* instructed. "Place the ring on Kai's finger and repeat after me."

Aiden took her left hand, listening carefully to the *kahu* then placed a lovely platinum band with three small sapphires onto her slightly shaking finger.

"Ali'ikai Leilani Kapahu, with this ring I thee wed," Aiden repeated confidently, smiling the entire time.

"Kai, do the same and repeat after me," the *kahu* requested.

When she was ready, the holy man repeated the phrase that would legally bind them.

"Aiden Joseph Kaplan, with this ring I thee wed," her voice was weak and shaky with emotion.

The wedding official smiled.

"With the power vested in me by the great state of Hawaii, I now pronounce you husband and wife." The man waggled his thick eyebrows making the audience laugh. "Now, you may kiss your bride."

Without further ado, Aiden pulled her into his arms and kissed her until her toes curled and all sensation in her lips disappeared. When he finally released her she had to lean against him to regain her equilibrium.

In a loud, clear voice the wedding official announced that they were now joined.

"It is my honor to introduce Mr. and Mrs. Aiden Kaplan!"

Aiden studied the beachside restaurant overlooking Waikiki Beach with admiration. Kai's family had done a beautiful job. The large main dining room was decorated like they were expecting *King Kamehameha* himself, with alternating plum, pink, and white calla floral centerpieces. Each table set with full china and silverware wrapped in white linen napkins and crystal water goblets as well as champagne flutes. Low frosted-glass votives, already lit, gave the room a soft, romantic glow. Toward the front of the main room, a single table set similarly, just for the two of them topped it all off.

The food looked amazing as well. The delicious smelling buffet consisted of Hawaiian dishes such as poi, Kalua pig, teriyaki beef, steamed white rice, potato salad, Asian-barbeque chicken, fried coconut shrimp specifically requested by their son, vegetable chow-mien and her uncle's famous Hawaiian sweet rolls, which he was addicted to, was making his stomach growl.

However, the wedding cake was the main centerpiece, a four-tiered confection with handmade, sugar callas adorning the top layer and cascading down one side. It could have been featured on a food television cake competition. Uncle Choy had outdone himself. It was the best wedding present he could have given them. The downfall of such a labor-intensive edible work of art which took an entire week to bake, assemble, and decorate, according to Kai's uncle, made the baker quite proud and also very demanding. Uncle Choy kept hinting that a creation like the one he had made deserved something extra special in return. Aiden promised to take him out on a destroyer as soon as he could arrange it.

Suddenly, he felt a hard slap on the back, looked over and saw Paul Choy, his long-time friend and now cousin-in-law. "Welcome to the family, man." Paul shook his hand firmly.

"Thanks, dude," he said, blushing the entire time.

"Who would have ever thought we'd," Paul gestured wildly between them. "Be related?"

"Certainly not me," Aiden scoffed. "Just kidding, *cuz!*"

Unexpectedly, he was put in a bear-hug and looked up into a dark face with a broad smile.

"Congratulations, brother!" Marcus released him from his powerful vise-like embrace. "It's about time you settled down. You're blessed to have her."

"I sure am," he agreed, glancing in his bride's direction.

"And you better treat my baby sister right or I'll kick your ass," Koa exclaimed loudly as he came to stand beside Paul. "Have you talked to her about the opportunity back on the mainland?" Koa asked.

The groom rubbed his nape trying to figure out how to tell Kai he'd been offered a teaching position at the Naval Academy in Maryland and had already accepted.

"No, I haven't. How do I convince her to give up her career and her family to move to Annapolis? She's gonna kill me."

"She's your family now," Marcus stated confidently. "Y'all will figure it out,"

"I hope so," he mumbled, unsure of his wife's reaction.

"Marcus, when are you and Vanessa heading back to Maryland?" Paul changed the subject when he noticed Aiden's panicked expression.

"After the baby is born, she's a week overdue. We plan on staying in Oahu for another three months and then we'll be back stateside. Tell you the truth though, I really love it here," he said honestly.

Aiden scanned the room for his wife. *Damn!* He had a wife and not just any wife, but his lovely Hawaiian flower. He was a proud, proud man.

Glancing around the room, he spotted her near the dance floor talking to her bridesmaids and a few relatives he had yet to meet.

"Excuse me gentlemen, but I have a wife to kiss."

Silently, he snuck up behind her, and grabbed her around her nipped-in waist.

"Hey," he whispered in her ear so only she could hear. "You look good enough to eat, *Mrs. Kaplan.*"

"When can we get out of here?" he questioned as he kissed her playfully below her earlobe.

When he glanced back up, all of the other women had disappeared.

"Behave, I'm only planning on getting married once and I want to enjoy it for as long as possible. We haven't even eaten yet, or cut the cake, or had our first dance as a married couple." She tiptoed to brush their lips together. "I'll make it up to you later."

She reached around and grabbed his ass with both hands.

"We can always hide in a supply closet or something."

He chuckled when she rolled her eyes.

"You'll have to wait until *later*," she rebuked, shaking her head.

"It starts already," he smirked, pulling her more snugly against his uniform-clad body.

Aiden couldn't stop looking at her. Her gown was simple, but elegant…unique, and she wore minimal make-up allowing her natural beauty to shine through. He wanted to scoop her up like *Richard Geer* in *An Officer and a Gentleman* and whisk her away to their honeymoon, but instead he practiced patience.

"Do you know what you do to me?" He nudged her with his groin, pressing the unnaturally hard flesh into the softness of her hip.

She felt so soft, so curvaceous, so *his*.

Slowly, he ran his hands down her bare arms, along her torso, over her hips, then back up, bending his knees to whisper extremely naughty things in her ear. Kai's body tensed. Breath hitched on a soft exhale, and he wanted her…right now.

"C'mon, baby, you know you want to sneak off and f—"

"Break it up you two." Her friend, Evelyn pulled them apart. "You're gonna set off the sprinkler system." Her words made him laugh.

"You must be Evelyn." He offered his hand. "I've heard a lot about you."

Evelyn hitched an eyebrow in Kai's direction.

"Well, ain't that a blip!" Evelyn ogled him from head to toe. "'cause I haven't heard much about you, Lieutenant Kaplan."

"Hmm." She ran her hand flirtatiously down his arm, stopping to squeeze his muscular biceps. "Kai, why didn't you tell me you were marrying Steve McGarrett?"

"Who?" Kai looked confused, and so did he.

"Tsk, tsk, tsk…you know the main character in Hawaii Five-O. What's that actor's name again… oh yeah, Alex O'Loughlin. Aiden, baby, you look like his twin, all tall and hard, and firmly packed. That man's sweeter than cotton candy and twice as addictive. If I were twenty years younger, I'd give your wife a run for her money."

"I'm sure you would, Evelyn," he blushed then Aiden gave her a brief hug. Not surprised when she grabbed his ass. "Whoa! Evelyn, I'm a married man now. You can look, but you can't touch."

"Uh huh." She kissed Kai on the cheek. "You did well. Maybe I can rent *this* one out." She waggled her brows, turned and sauntered over to the buffet.

Kai covered her mouth trying desperately to confine the laughter getting ready to erupt.

"She's one of a kind. You'll get use to her."

"I love her already."

"You did a great job on the wedding." Aiden kissed her left cheek. "And the reception." And then kissed her right cheek. "*Mrs. Kaplan.*"

"Mahalo," she smirked, loving his playfulness.

"Kinda surreal, isn't it."

"It is," she giggled then stared into space.

"What?" Aiden stopped to gaze loving at her.

"I don't think I'll ever get use to that," Kai admitted as she snuggled against her wonderfully naked hunk of a husband. *"Mrs. Kai Kapahu-Kaplan."*

"What do you think of us getting A.J.'s last name formally changed to Kaplan but keep Kapahu as one of his middle names?" he suggested with all sincerity.

"Aiden Joseph Kapahu Kaplan."

She tested the sound on her tongue.

"I love it!" she purred, then hugged him tightly. "We should do it as soon as possible."

"Good!" That all too familiar feeling of pride threatening to burst from his chest as he admired his bride.

"What else did you want to tell me?" she added with an omniscient tone.

"Huh?"

"Out with it," she urged. "You've been stressing about something the entire day. Spill it."

"Still so bossy," he teased, preparing for her reaction.

"Spill it sailor," she repeated.

"Ok, ok, don't hurt me."

He wasn't exactly joking. His wife had a mean right hook.

"I've been offered a teaching position at the Naval Academy in Annapolis," he blurted. "I've already accepted it."

He closed his eyes, bracing for a punch, but it never came. Slowly, he opened his eyes. Kai was sitting up beside him on the large king-sized bed in their Maui honeymoon cottage, her face a blank slate.

"But you haven't even discussed it with me," she stated calmly, pulling the thin white sheet up to cover her breasts.

"The officer who was supposed to do it pulled out at the last minute," he divulged. "I had to make a decision quickly."

"I thought you were putting in for a transfer to Pearl-Hickam for the lead engineering position that way you'd only have to travel once in a while?"

"The other offer was better for my career," he educated gingerly. "I had to make a fast decision, otherwise, someone else would have grabbed it. It's a once-in-a-lifetime opportunity, Kai."

Exasperated, she turned to him, tears welling.

"It would have taken you a few minutes to call me, explain the situation, and figure it out…*together*. That's what couples do, Aiden."

"I know I messed-up." He sat up, circling her shoulders with one arm, glad she didn't push him away. "I'm sorry. I should have never made the decision without talking to you first."

"Damn right!" Kai felt her blood pressure rising as she stared into the face of a man who was totally clueless to the degree of his fuck up.

"I'm sorry," he pleaded. "It'll never happen again. I promise."

"It better not," she huffed as the tension bounced between them in waves. "You have to include me in every decision, otherwise this won't work."

"I know. I won't make any more life altering decisions without you." He tugged her back down on top of his smooth chest. "I promise."

His kisses were soft along her neck and shoulders, and she couldn't contain the moan that escaped her lips.

"When do we have to move back to the mainland?" she sighed on a moan.

Aiden kissed his way down her body until he arrived at her right nipple. He greeted it with a slow, wet glide before sucking it into the warm cavern of his mouth. The traitorous bud instantly hardened into a stiff point under his expert ministrations.

"I have to be back no later than the first week of June." His mouth seduced her until she was ready to melt into the comforter.

"That's right around the corner, Aiden."

She felt the tension leaving her limbs under his expert touch.

"Mmm," he mumbled. "This nipple is so tasty."

"I'm still angry with you," she yelped when he gently bit her hardened peak then soothed the sting with another sensuous lick.

"I know but let me make it up to you."

With that promise, her husband rolled her over and made slow, passionate love to her.

CHAPTER TWELVE

Kai gaped unable to form a coherent sentence, taking-in the luxurious surroundings. When Aiden said he owned a townhouse, she immediately pictured a small, cramped, ugly, bachelor pad like he had in college. This place couldn't compare to her parents' house in Hawaii, but it was still stylish and comfortable and unlike his old apartment, didn't smell like dirty socks.

"This is really lovely," she stated, eyes widening with disbelief.

Chuckling, he ushered his wife and son into the foyer of his Annapolis home.

"Why are you so surprised I have a nice place?"

She tilted her head daring him to argue.

"Ok," he conceded. "My apartment back in the day was a bit—"

"Messy, stinky, hideous, revolting," she snickered. "Should I go on?"

"It wasn't that bad," he frowned.

"Wasn't that bad," she huffed. Her face contorted into an expression so hilarious he couldn't help the laughter bellowing out of his lungs.

The two bedrooms, two bath townhouse was immaculate to say the least. His living room furnishings consisted of a full-sized sofa and matching recliner, glass coffee table and of course a gigantic sixty-inch, flat-screen television. A custom-made shelving unit along the entire back wall of the living room housed a variety of books ranging from the official biography of Nelson Mandela to James Patterson's latest thriller, vintage vinyl records including old-school Louis Armstrong to indie rock, a huge collection of *Blu-ray*, and handmade trinkets, vases, and tribal masks he had collected from his travels around the world adorned the shelves.

She let out a low whistle. "Color me impressed," she mumbled under her breath.

"Daddy, may I watch TV?" A.J. plopped down on the couch.

"You don't want the grand tour?"

"No, thanks, maybe later," his son made himself comfortable.

Aiden smiled turning back to Kai.

"I guess it's just you and me," he winked at his obviously impressed new bride.

Haphazardly, he deposited their suitcases near the foyer, taking her by the hand, and then led her past the living room to another area. To the left of the living space was a brightly lit modern kitchen, fully outfitted with stainless steel appliances, a well-organized walk-in pantry, large farmhouse sink, granite countertops and beautiful cherry wood cabinets. It was a professional chef's dream space.

"Do you cook often?" she asked, curious about his life pre-marriage.

"Not as much as I'd like to, but now I'm sure that will change."

He tapped the end of her nose with his slightly calloused finger. The contact instantly sending a tingle of arousal through to her core. Blissfully, she wandered examining the beautiful space, smiling with thoughts of cooking meals for her newly-formed family.

Quite unexpectedly, a sudden pang of nausea hit her, and she had to lean against the counter to keep her balance. Aiden rushed to her side, panic blanketing his handsome features.

"What's wrong? Do you need some crackers or something?" he frowned.

He was running around grumbling to himself and looking quite crazed.

"Shit! I don't have anything here," he grumbled to himself. "I emptied the fridge before I left...let me check the pantry. I might have some in there. Crackers don't spoil do they?"

"Aiden, sweetheart," her gentle tone seemed to calm his nerves. "You can't panic every time I throw up or get dizzy. You'll have a heart attack."

Pulling her into his arms, his breathing began to return to normal.

"Is it normal having morning sickness during the second trimester?" Kai noticed they no longer fit perfectly together because of her baby bump.

"For me it is," she reassured as he held her, stroking her back with comforting motions. "You better stop. You're making me hot and remember it was in a similar room you did *this* to me."

She chuckled pointing to her belly.

He chuckled too.

"Maybe when our son goes to bed we can christen this room," he teased, his waggling eyebrows making her laugh.

From over his shoulder, Kai noticed the cookbooks. Several of them in fact, stacked neatly on a shelf in the built-in desk/computer console in the far corner of the kitchen. Curious, she wandered over to read the titles.

"You weren't joking about learning how to cook from the Food Network," she giggled. "You've got everyone from Rachael Ray to Guy Fieri over here."

"Let me give you the rest of the tour."

Taking her hand once again, he led her out of the kitchen and into the living room where A.J. was still trying to figure out how to use the remote for the television.

"Are you okay, buddy? Need some help?" Aiden queried.

"It's alright, Daddy," the intelligent child reassured. "I like figuring stuff out."

"If you need us, I'll be showing your mom where everything is," he grinned proudly.

A.J. nodded and went back to tinkering with the rather large remote control.

Enthralled by her new surroundings, Kai held her husband's hand and walked around the two-level unit as Aiden showed her the laundry room and den/office, then crossed back to the living room.

"Behind these French doors is a balcony, nothing fancy, but it's pleasant to sit outside when the weather is nice," he explained, knowing his wife would probably enjoy the space when the weather allowed.

Maryland in early June was hot and humid, even with the slight breeze coming in from the Chesapeake. She knew both she and A.J. would miss the temperate weather of Honolulu, but she hoped she'd find it bearable or at least tolerate it, for Aiden's sake.

"June to mid-September is hot, but after that the temperature gets cooler and the leaves start to change color…and…"

Kai playfully pinched his arm.

"Honey, I'm sure I'll love it," she reassured. "Stop worrying so much."

He nodded then turned back to face the living area.

"There isn't a formal dining area just the eat-in kitchen which you've already seen."

"This place is much larger than I expected," she gave a genuine smile.

Upstairs there were two bedrooms. The smaller room he used for guests, but she knew he hadn't had any guests, except them.

"A.J. can sleep in here." He flipped on the overhead light so she could get a better look. "A little later, after you've rested, we can run up to the home goods store and pick-up some curtains and the superhero sheets he likes so much."

To her delight, it was a good-sized space with a full-sized bed, dresser, nightstand, small walk-in closet, and large window filling the room with soft afternoon sunlight.

"He'll love it!" she declared, confidently.

Unexpectedly, he picked her up like she weighed nothing at all and carried her, like the new bride she was, to the master suite.

"Down the hall is our room."

"Aiden," she giggled. "Put me down before you get a hernia."

He threw his head back, laughing in a deep baritone. When they arrived, he carefully stood her upright in the middle of the space.

"And this is our room." He stood motionless, studying her expression. "You don't like it?"

"No... I mean, yes," she asserted with a smile. "It's... kinda like a blank canvas... instead of well lived-in like the rest of the house."

It truly was blank and bland. The walls were painted in a neutral eggshell, but there were no pictures or art or any knick-knacks to make the room feel homey. There was a massive king-sized bed with matching headboard, dresser and two nightstands. An armoire housed a thirty-six-inch flat screen and iPod charging station, but other than that it was plain which her husband was anything but.

"This room doesn't reflect you at all," she informed, her gaze sweeping the space one more time, taking it all in.

Aiden bent his knees so he could look into her eyes, amber to blue.

"I guess I've been waiting for you to come and put your special touch on it...just like you did to my heart."

"Corn-dog," she smirked, then wrapped her arms around his waist, resting her cheek on his chest, his heart beating a steady tattoo.

"With you, always," he confessed then bent his head claiming her mouth with a heartfelt kiss.

Overjoyed, Kai breathed in the soothing scent of sandalwood and musk that was unique to him.

"Do you think there will be enough space when the baby comes?"

"We can buy something bigger, something nicer, maybe near the Chesapeake Bay." He pulled away a few inches to look at her face. "Would you like that?"

"I don't care where we are as long as we're together," Kai sighed, comforted in her husband's arms and she knew she was home.

Aiden chuckled as he entered their bedroom.

"I can't believe that boy has so much energy," he groaned. "He's making me feel like an old man."

"Is he finally asleep?" Kai watched his amused expression, laughter softening her amber gaze.

"Finally," he grinned recalling A.J.'s bedtime antics. "It took two stories and a glass of water before he drifted off."

"Welcome to the world of parenthood," his bride proclaimed.

His chuckle was low and husky.

"How's our little peanut doing?" he asked since Kai seemed at ease.

Peanut was their new nickname for the baby. Kai was in the second trimester of her pregnancy and other than an occasional bout of nausea and the constant need to pee and eat the most questionable mixture of foods, she was progressing nicely. Only problem was, according to his way of thinking, she hadn't been in the mood for sex… *at all*… and he was going to lose his mind.

Every time he looked at his wife, he wanted to jump her bones. And not in the romantic, let's make love way, but the nasty let's fuck like bunnies' kind of way. Was it his fault Kai was even more beautiful and desirable pregnant? Her skin more radiant due to the pregnancy hormones, her hair thicker and fuller than usual with a shiny bounce and her breasts… *Dear God!* Her breasts were fuller, rounder, and just…*more*. It seemed like any time she was in the same vicinity as he, his cock was on high-alert. It had gotten so bad he was now reduced to jacking-off in the shower at least twice a day. He could only imagine what their water bill would be like.

"Peanut, is just fine," She smiled touching her stomach. "How's Daddy doing?"

Aiden debated if he should tell her he was hornier than a dog in heat and if she'd let him, he'd be more than willing to hump her leg, but he decided against it.

"I'm tired," he responded, hoping she'd believe him.

One perfectly-shaped brow rose.

"Are you sure?" she frowned. "You look flushed."

"Do I?" he muttered.

"Yeah."

There was that eyebrow again.

"Huh," he grinned nervously.

Trying to avoid more questions, Aiden walked toward the bathroom undressing as he went, exhausted from the long trip from Honolulu to Annapolis.

"I'm gonna take a shower, be out in a minute."

Kai nodded, her lips slightly parted, chest rising and falling like she'd just exercised.

"Are *you* okay?" concern seeping into his words.

He had missed their first pregnancy, so he wasn't sure what to expect. Therefore, any action on Kai's part perceived to be irregular raised his hackles.

"*You* look a bit flushed."

She shook her head obviously amused with his apprehension.

"No, I'm fine," she swore as her intense gaze studied his now naked physique, tongue darting out caressing that distracting, full bottom lip.

Aiden felt his cock twitch and quickened his pace to the shower. Aiden didn't want her to think he was a complete sex-addict when it came to her, even if he was. Maybe he *would* jack-off in the shower to put himself out of his misery.

"I'll be back soon," he announced. Kai nodded again and he could feel her staring at his ass as he walked away. Realizing this, he tensed his gluts, smiling when he heard her breath hitch.

"You're such a tease, Lieutenant Kaplan," she called after him good-humoredly.

Closing the bathroom door behind him, he stood for a moment examining his reflection. He looked the same, dark hair, blue eyes, straight nose, squared jaw line, but internally he felt as giddy as a teenager and he knew it was because of the two, soon to be three, new additions to his once very uneventful life. Kai, Peanut, and A.J. were all blessings and he was determined to give them the lifestyle they deserved.

Robotically, Aiden adjusted the shower knobs until the water was set to the proper temperature. Not too hot. Not too cold. Exactly in the middle, just the way he preferred it. Stepping under the steady stream escaping from the multi-setting showerhead, Aiden felt the tension in his shoulders and back slipping away and down the drain. Grabbing the bottle of shower gel and a washcloth, he began lathering his neck, underarms, and torso, then reached behind him to finish his back and glutes. When he was done, he reached down grabbing his now painfully hard member. Holding it firmly at the shaft, he stroked it from root to tip, once…twice…

"Is this a private moment or can wives join in?" Kai stood gloriously naked at the entrance to the shower, inky spirals cascading past her toned shoulders, firm, heavy breasts beaded into tight peaks. Her smooth honey-colored skin shining with a healthy inner glow. Her beauty had always taken his breath away, but knowing she carried his child made her even more beautiful. Aiden felt a wave of emotion wash over him and he suddenly needed her more than he could bear.

"How long have you been standing there ogling my goodies?" his teasing tone causing her to blush.

"Not long, but I was definitely enjoying the show," she snorted jokingly making his cock flex again.

He smiled at her playfulness.

"You already took a shower."

She smirked, letting her hands move up to cup her full, ripe breasts, slowly circling the cocoa-hued areolas with her thumbs.

"But I'm still so...*dirty*." She pinched both hard buds. "I need you to clean me up."

He gulped, hard, unable to remove his gaze from her.

"Get in here, sexy."

He took her hand and helped her inside, tugging her gently against the hard contours of his body. With her growing belly, they didn't fit together the way they usually did, but it still felt like it was meant to be...natural.

"I was just thinking about you," he confessed.

Aiden ran his hands over the sides of her torso feeling the dips and valleys of his wife's curvaceous form.

"Yeah?" She swallowed hard, breath coming in delicate pants. "What were you thinking about me? Was it something naughty?"

She reached around to his back and followed the path down to his ass, grabbing both cheeks and kneading firmly.

"Mmm," she sighed. "You have a body made for sin."

"Said the kettle to the pot," he corrected.

Needing to gaze into her eyes, Aiden bent his knees, so they were now at eye level. Her amber irises were sparkling with desire and his cock responded by hardening another couple of inches.

"I was thinking about these." He moved both hands to lovingly palm her large, firm breasts using his thumbs to gently flick her chocolate-colored peaks.

"Pig," she taunted, her breathing accelerating; a low moan rushed out as she arched her back, pushing her breasts more securely into his hands.

"And this," he added, gliding his left hand away from her breast, over her raised stomach, through the neatly-trimmed dark curls to cup her sopping, wet mound. Before she could respond, he slipped his middle finger into her entrance.

"Always so wet for me." His jaw clenched as she tightened her inner muscles around his thick digit. "And so friggin tight…so good."

Once again, he found her lips and continued to push into the damp cavern, finding her tongue and greeting it with several long, wet swipes.

"Aiden," she moaned into his mouth, the sensation making his legs tremble.

"I want you so badly," he whispered against her mouth then added another finger to her sex, still pumping in the slow, unhurried tempo. "This sweet pussy is killing me."

"Oh," was her only response to his devastating movements.

Next, his thumb found her clit, hard and peeking out from under its hood, begging for attention. Using gentle pressure, he drew invisible circles over the slippery nubbin. The action causing Kai to open her legs greedily as she rocked against his hand.

"Yeah, just like that…fuck my hand you dirty, dirty girl."

"Oh…oh!" Her body tensed, eyes squeezed shut, and he knew what was quickly approaching.

"That's it." He kissed her gently, so in contrast with his fast-moving fingers. "I can't wait to have your cream all over me."

"Aiden," she whimpered. "I'm gonna come!"

Immediately, he quickened his motions, fingers moving in and out of her pussy at a frenzied pace.

"Come for me, Kai."

The orgasm hit her hard enough to make her knees buckle. When she reached, Aiden eased his wife away from his body, out of the direct line of the shower spray, leaning her still vibrating body onto the cold shower tiles.

"That was amazing," she whispered, her body still pulsating with the aftershocks.

"I'm not done with you," his arrogant grin promised more wicked delights.

Without warning, he knelt in front of her and using both of his thumbs, Aiden parted her nether lips and ran the tip of his tongue along the inner edge of the slick opening, avoiding her most sensitive area. His wife writhed with pleasure, thrusting her pelvis at his face. Aiden licked her pussy like an ice cream cone, knowing her approaching release would be much more intense if he took his time. She had already climaxed a few moments before, but he wanted the second time to be equally pleasurable.

"Oh, my gracious," Kai moaned, her voice strained with need.

"Feel good, baby?" he asked, but not really expecting an answer.

"Hell yeah," she uttered almost incoherently.

Looking away from her heated stare, Aiden lowered his head to her pussy again, sucking her throbbing nubbin into his mouth. He tightened his grip on her supple thighs, trying to maintain his quickly fleeing control. A groan escaped him, the vibration making her inner walls contract, as he plunged two fingers inside her, finding her G-spot and stroking her to near madness.

"Aiden!" she screamed, and he hoped their son couldn't hear her from his room down the hall.

Doubling his efforts, he began stroking her juicy cunt with his pumping fingers while nipping and sucking her clit. He felt that now familiar tightening of her vaginal walls and knew exactly when she climaxed… forcefully… all over his eagerly lapping tongue.

At last, he stood, legs shaking with his own desire to find release.

"Turn around, face the wall for me."

He smiled when she followed his order without hesitation.

"Put your hands flat against the wall. If you move, I'll stop," his statement confident, even if his body wasn't. "Do you understand?"

She nodded.

"Open those sexy legs," his voice was laced with excitement. "Yeah, just like that."

"I need you," she moaned.

Gently, he kissed her temple.

"You'll have me soon enough," he promised.

"Hurry!"

"Push this sweet ass back…a little bit more. Oh God…that's it. Don't move."

Kai shivered at his command, wiggling her backside, taunting him.

"I'm gonna fuck you so good; you won't remember your name," he growled low in his throat.

"Promises… promises," she teased.

A heartbeat later, Kai's entrance was prodded by his irresistibly thick rod. Desperately, Aiden clenched his jaw trying to prolong his climax as it barreled down on him. Increasing his pace, he pounded into her silky folds. Cursing under his breath at the ecstasy he found within the tight space. Kai's pussy tightened around his cock, and he knew she was having another orgasm.

"Fuck! I'm coming already," he announced as jets of hot semen shot inside her channel. The force of it making him slightly dizzy… overwhelmed…and loved.

After a few moments of kissing and caressing, they washed away the evidence of their lovemaking, dried off and a few minutes later lay in the massive king-sized bed. Exhausted after their shower Olympics, his wife tucked her body against his side, breasts smashed against him.

Concerned he wasn't able to control his lust as well as he'd hoped, he asked, "Are you feeling sore?"

"Nope," she laughed. "I guess you must be losing your touch in your old age."

A dark brow arched up.

"Excuse me?" he scoffed with a wry little smile. "Did you just imply I wasn't up to par?"

"It's nothing to worry about," she jabbed with mock empathy. "I heard it happens to lots of men your age."

"Men my age? Men *my* age," he chuckled. "I'm only twenty-nine."

"Hey," she stated flatly. "You're the one who said you were old."

"I was joking," he chuckled.

Kai tapped her finger on her lips thoughtfully.

"Maybe you should buy some vitamins," she suggested with a mischievous grin. "It might improve your performance. After all, you only gave me two orgasms."

"No," he denied, shaking his head as he spoke. "Three."

"What?"

"I gave you three orgasms," he waggled his eyebrows suggestively.

"You must be mistaken." Kai sat up suddenly.

"Nope, it was three," he sung the words like a child singing a nursery rhyme.

"I didn't know you were keeping count." She smacked him playfully.

"Yup, I gave you three Earth-shattering orgasms, *three*, to my *one*," he informed smugly.

"We can't have that," she informed as she straddled his hips, groin to groin.

Sitting up on her knees to get more height, she reached back grabbing his swollen member and lined it up to her dripping slit. He tensed when she lowered herself just enough to lodge the weeping mushroom-head of his cock into her channel. Her inner muscles gripped him with vise-like strength almost bringing him to release with the contact.

She was just about to complete their joining when they both heard a knock at the door.

"Mommy... Daddy?"

"Damn it!" he mouthed to Kai, who tried to dislodge him from her body, but he held her securely. "If we don't say anything he might go back to bed."

She shook her head.

"He's stubborn like his daddy and he's not going anywhere until he gets what he wants."

"Shush." He pressed a finger to her lips. "He'll hear you."

"Mommy?" A.J. wiggled the doorknob. Thank goodness he had remembered to lock the door.

"Yeah, buddy?" Kai answered.

Aiden's member instantly began to soften.

"May I have a glass of water, please?"

"Sure, I'll be right there."

Slowly, she got off of his lap, going to the walk-in closet to find her robe.

"Daddy?"

"What's up, son?" his jaw clenched as he admired her nakedness.

"Can *you* get me some water?"

He smiled proudly knowing his son requested him instead of his mother.

"Okay."

Swiftly, Aiden rolled out of bed pulling on the jeans he had left on the carpeted floor of the room. When he turned back toward the bed, Kai was already snuggling under the soft gray comforter, smiling to herself.

"Don't fall asleep or else." he growled, a lecherous grin invading his features as she smiled to herself.

"Or else what?" she giggled, closing her eyes in pure defiance.

"Believe me, you'll find out," he joked.

Needing to leave before he was tempted to return to bed and have his way with her, he opened the door and found his son sitting quietly on the floor, leaning against the wall, a sleepy smile appearing when he spotted him. Immediately, Aiden bent and scooped up his little boy into a fireman's hold.

"You need some water?"

A.J. shook his wavy locks.

Silently, they went down to the kitchen, drank some water then made their way back to A.J.'s room. Earlier in the evening, they had visited a local home goods store and purchased a few items to decorate the space. A.J. chose a *Superman* bed-in-a-bag with matching curtain panels, a few comic book style posters to decorate the walls, some games, books and toys, and a bean-bag chair just for a fun place to sit. Even with just a few new accessories, the room looked like it was always meant to be a child's haven.

Filled with parental pride, Aiden tucked his son back into bed and read him one of the new storybooks. When he thought the boy would never fall asleep, A.J. yawned, closed his eyes and laid his head on his father's chest.

"Don't leave," his son pleaded.

"Do you want me to stay with you until you fall asleep?"

A.J. nodded.

Reaching over, he turned off the bed-side lamp then snuggled under the covers with his son close beside him. Overly tired and sated from lovemaking, Aiden closed his eyes, enjoying the serenity of the moment.

"Goodnight, A.J." He placed a kiss on the little boy's forehead.

"Goodnight, Daddy."

And they quickly drifted off to sleep.

❦

Kai awoke the next morning alone in a strange room. Panic-stricken she sat up. Sweeping a confused gaze over the contents of the room. After a minute or so, she realized she was in Aiden's bedroom… in Annapolis. Quickly, she got up, put on her robe, and headed to the bathroom to freshen-up. After brushing her teeth, washing her face and putting her hair up into a messy ponytail, she made her way down the hall to A.J.'s room. Surprisingly, the room was empty even though it was barely light outside. Concerned, she glanced at the alarm clock on the nightstand…seven o'clock. She wondered where they were so early in the morning.

As gracefully as she could with a growing belly, she made a quick examination of the upstairs before heading to the lower level. Downstairs in the kitchen, she found her two men busy cooking breakfast. There was stuff everywhere: eggshells, melted butter, an opened milk carton, and a medley of pans and utensils all over the once-clean granite countertops.

"Good morning, Mommy," her son greeted as she placed a quick kiss to his cheek.

"Morning, little man."

Then she turned to her husband, kissed him chastely on his sinful mouth and smacked him playfully on the ass.

"Morning, big guy," she flirted, waggling her brows at his surprise. "I thought you were coming back to get your second…"

A.J. looked at them curiously.

"…dessert," she blushed.

Her husband chuckled.

"I had every intention to come back for my…*dessert*, but your son wanted me to sleep with him."

"I see." She kissed him again. "I waited and waited, all by my lonesome."

"Poor baby."

He reached around to grab her ass, but noticed their son's innocent face looked at them like they were crazy.

Kai winked and went to the fridge to retrieve the bottle of orange juice they had bought the night before.

"What's for breakfast?" She tried ignoring the mess. "It smells delicious."

"Daddy and I are making French toast with bacon," their child informed. "We thought Peanut would like it."

"Sounds good," she said then sipped her juice. "What are our plans today?"

"I thought we could go down to the Naval Academy and I could give you a tour of the campus and show you my new office," he relayed. "We can have lunch in the cafeteria. Does that sound alright?"

"Sounds good to me," she answered truthfully. "Before I forget, I have to call my parents to let them know we reached safely, and everything is fine. I also have to check-up with Vanessa to see if she's delivered already, and I'll need to find an OBGYN soon… and I also—"

"Maybe you should make a list that way we don't forget anything," Aiden interrupted her rant.

"Terrific idea," she agreed.

"Breakfast is ready," A.J. announced.

"Good, let's eat and then I'll help you guys' clean-up this mess."

The Naval Academy was incredible, from the well-maintained grounds to the meticulously-kept buildings. It was just as he'd remembered. He had always loved being on campus and loved the idea of imparting knowledge to the next generation of military leaders. Not to mention, following in his father's footsteps.

"I'm impressed, Aiden." Kai squeezed his hand.

"It is impressive, isn't it?" It wasn't a question.

"I can't believe you're going to be teaching…here," she complimented as she kissed his chin. "I couldn't be more proud."

"Daddy, I'm going to come here for college too."

"You are?" Aiden picked up their son and settled him down on the brand-new brown leather office chair.

A.J. nodded and pretended to type something on the keyboard.

"Are you going to be an engineer like me?"

"Yes, sir," he grinned. "Or I might be a physical therapist like Mommy…or a fireman like Conrad's dad…or maybe a superhero…"

Aiden chuckled to himself.

"Those sound like really great careers, A.J.," Aiden winked. "What about you, Mommy? Do you like it?"

"I love your office," she agreed, glancing around the small, yet efficient space.

He had to admit it wasn't much to look at. The room, sparsely furnished, contained a solid oak desk, office chair, two matching brown leather armchairs, desk lamp, telephone, printer, computer, monitor and keyboard, wall clock, and built-in bookshelves along three sides. A large palladium window overlooking the commons below made the room seem larger and more inviting.

"It just needs a few personal touches to really make it yours," Kai concluded, studying the room once more.

"I agree," he beamed.

"Me too," A.J. added. "We can get some more superhero posters for you to put up in here."

Aiden couldn't help the laugh that forced its way out.

"Yup, that would definitely make it my space."

A knock on the office door drew their attention. Before Aiden could open it a very handsome man in his mid-fifties stepped inside, wearing a standard Navy service uniform, his hat securely under his arm, and leather satchel draped over his left shoulder. Aiden glanced at his wife before standing at full-attention saluting respectfully.

"At ease, lieutenant." The man smiled, but it didn't reach his eyes. Stepping forward, he offered his hand and Aiden shook it stiffly. "How are you?"

"Fine, sir," Aiden responded without emotion.

"Congratulations on your new assignment," the other man stated flatly.

"Thank you, sir."

"I hope you realize the significance of this teaching position, Lieutenant Kaplan," the senior officer added.

"I do, sir," Aiden replied awkwardly, his eyes darkening.

"You look well, son. Married life must be agreeing with you." The man turned to her, right hand outstretched as he added, "And you must be the little woman."

Aiden stepped beside her placing an arm around her waist and pulling her firmly against him.

"This is Kai," he introduced mechanically. "Kai, this is Admiral John Aiden Kaplan, my father."

He could tell Kai wasn't surprised, other than his salt-and-pepper locks and two-inch height differential, Aiden was the spitting image of his father, right down to the wicked gleam in their gray-blue eyes.

"It's a pleasure to meet you, sir." Kai shook his hand with a firm grip that seemed to surprise and impress the admiral.

"Please, call me John," he said a bit uneasily. "I've heard a lot about you, young lady. My son's been enamored with you since the day he met you."

Her cheeks flushed when she glanced over at Aiden, who struggled to contain his anger.

"And now that I've seen you, I know why." John winked at his son whose hands were clenched into fists at his sides.

Next, his father turned to A.J., who was staring up at him, smiling in his usual self-confident manner.

"And who is this young man?"

Aiden stood a little taller, more defiant.

"You know exactly who this is." Aiden turned to A.J. "Son, this is your grandfather. Sir, meet Aiden Joseph Kapahu Kaplan…your grandson."

Without missing a beat, the admiral squatted to speak with A.J., blue eyes to blue eyes.

"It's nice to meet you, Aiden."

"Glad to meet you too, sir," the boy spoke, then shook his grandfather's hand.

Aiden cleared his throat.

"We call him A.J."

"Okay." His father smiled and for a brief moment he could see himself in twenty-some-odd years, looking like the man in front of them. "A.J. it is."

"What should I call you?" A.J. questioned.

"I have a few choice names," Aiden mumbled.

His father looked at him but did not respond.

"I don't know, but I'm sure we'll figure it out."

Then he stood and turned back to Aiden.

"You have a fine family, Lieutenant Kaplan," his father said brightly. "Don't mess it up."

Aiden saw Kai grimace and he felt the heat in his own face spread as he stepped forward.

His wife spoke first.

"Thank you, sir," her look chastising. "I mean, John. The Naval Academy is impressive, to say the least. I'm sure Aiden will love teaching here."

She smiled, trying to ease the tension growing between him and his asshole of a father.

"Yes, it's an impressive position to hold for a man of his age and rank," John placated.

"He's always wanted to follow in your footsteps," Kai agreed.

"Thank you, and what do you do young lady…I mean besides my son."

Before Kai could respond, he stepped between them.

"Sir, may I speak to you in private," his words were terse and provocative, and the sound of his voice was harsh even to his own ears.

The other man bristled.

"Of course," John spoke as if he had done nothing wrong. "Kai, A.J. it was very nice to meet you."

"Nice to meet you too, John," she responded with a forced smile.

"Goodbye, sir." A.J. waved.

Aiden kissed her on the cheek before leaning down to her ear and whispering.

"My father's office is four doors down to the left. It's the room right before the elevators," he directed. "I'll be right back."

Then he turned to A.J.

"Stay here with Mommy," he requested. "Daddy will be right back."

"Yes, sir." A.J. looked at him lovingly and he could feel some of the tension leave his limbs.

With much difficulty, Aiden held his tongue during the short walk to his father's office, but as soon as the door was closed behind him his blood boiled over and there was no way of stopping it.

"You fucking, cock-sucking asshole!" Aiden barked, fighting the urge to punch the other man on the nose. "How could you not tell me Kai was pregnant with my kid, you son-of-a-bitch?"

"Calm down, sailor." His father sat in his office chair seemingly unaffected by his tirade.

"How could you have kept that information to yourself?" Aiden's voice loudened.

"I didn't want you to ruin your future!" John snapped back.

"Ruin my future?!" he spat vehemently. "Explain yourself."

"Do you think I wanted my only child getting married to some little island tart?" the other man growled menacingly. "Possibly throwing away a successful military career in the process. For what? A piece of ass? Even though, I have to admit, it's a mighty fine ass."

"Shut the hell up!"

Aiden slammed his fists down on the large mahogany desk causing the picture frames to fall over and the pencil holder to topple, spilling its contents onto the hardwood floors. It took all of his will-power not to leap over the desk and pummel the smug look right off of the admiral's face.

"If you ever call her that again or make any disparaging remarks about her, I'll beat the shit out of you. I don't care if the military police haul me away to the brig, just the satisfaction of wiping that look off of your face would keep me happy for the next fifty years."

Then he turned to leave, anger fueling his movements.

"Was it worth it?" His father's angry glare halted his movement toward the exit.

"What are you talking about?"

"All this, getting married, having a family?" His father's tone was hollow. "You were supposed to make the Navy your first priority. What happened?"

Aiden was just about to answer when the door slowly opened.

"I'm sorry to disturb you." Kai poked her head inside, her features tense with worry. "I knocked, but no one answered."

"What's the matter?" his tone quickly softened.

It was then that he noticed that his wife was rubbing her belly, a nervous action Aiden had become used to.

"Is the baby okay?" he frowned, completely disregarding his father. "Are you ok?"

"I'm feeling a bit tired and A.J. is ready for lunch," she told with an anxious expression.

"The two of you are expecting...*again*?" his father questioned dryly.

Kai stood straighter, shoulders pushed back defiantly, eyes expressionless.

"Aiden, could you please take A.J. to the bathroom? He's waiting in the hallway right outside the door."

A confused expression appeared as he glanced from the man sitting behind the desk to his lovely Hawaiian bride and suddenly felt sorry for the admiral.

"Of course," he replied. "I'll be right back."

She nodded, smiling grimly.

As he exited, he pulled the door closed behind him, took his son by the hand leading the way to the nearest restroom. Hopefully, when he returned, he wouldn't find his father's lifeless body tossed out the window or laying in a bloody heap. No amount of military training could save the man now.

Kai heard the door shut, saw the man in front of her settle back in his chair, and knew it was time to do what she had sworn to do from the time Aiden had spoken about his father's lack of interest in him. This wasn't about her, well not entirely. She had convinced herself that it was about telling the smug, ass-hat of a man what she thought of him.

"Congratulations," he mocked while taking inventory of her.

"For what?" her tone was clipped.

"For the nuptials, of course. It took some time, but you finally wrangled my boy into marrying you. I'm sure you're proud of yourself…hooking a wealthy naval officer and all," he nodded to her baby-bump. "Also sealing the deal with a new child was clever."

"Thank you, sir," she stated unemotionally. "I'm honored you find me so cunning and manipulative."

Without being invited, Kai sat on one of the custom-made black suede wing-back chairs facing his desk.

"Considering, I'm a lowly Hawaiian *tart*, who would have thought I'd have that much influence over a highly educated, devastatingly handsome lieutenant who had women drooling at his feet, but decided to marry someone who hadn't made any contact with him for over six years," she rambled then rapidly composed herself.

"You must have worked some kind of island magic on him," John retorted calmly, egging her on.

"Oh, I did," she continued. "I treated him with respect and supported him emotionally instead of always putting him down or making him feel like a stranger instead of—"

"Who do think you are speaking to?!"

"I'm speaking to a man who is too stupid to see what an amazing son he has," she chastised as calmly as she could. "All Aiden has ever wanted from you is for you to be proud of him, but for some reason you can't see him for the wonderful person he is."

John's features darkened.

"What makes you think you know him so well?" her father-in-law babbled, losing his composure. "Being friends in college doesn't make you an expert on him, Mrs. Kaplan. You don't realize—"

Kai arched her brow at him, giving him her mother's "look of death" stare causing him to stop mid-sentence, eyes wide like saucers, mouth slightly opened.

"I find this amusing coming from a man who didn't have the common decency to attend his own son's college graduation or come to check on him after he had knee surgery and was devastated to learn he might never be able to play basketball again," she verbally slapped his self-righteous attitude out of the way.

"You have no right speaking to me this way," he snarled, cheeks red.

Unafraid, she leaned closer to his desk, resting her folded hands on the beautifully polished wood surface.

"These nasty, hateful things from a man who abandoned his grieving teenager when his mother died. This from a man who found out he was going to be a grandfather and didn't care to inform his own son of that fact," she countered forcefully. "I wonder what your wife would think of the man you have become."

Stunned at her fearlessness, John sat back, a strange look on his face she didn't recognize. His mouth pressed into a thin, harsh line. Eyes wide open in shock.

"And you are right, about one thing," she said, continuing to look directly at those darkening baby blues. "I am lucky to have married him. I'd never be able to find someone more loving, more thoughtful, more ambitious, and more honorable than your son."

Finally she stood, slowly turned toward the door, and then paused in midstride to glance over her shoulder at him.

"I guess he must have learned those qualities from his mother."

Aiden abandoned the bench he and A.J. were currently sitting on when his wife appeared. Immediately, he stood, and waited for her to tell him what had happened with his father. He hoped she hadn't gotten in a physical altercation with the other man, although he was positive Kai could take him.

"Everything alright?" her husband prodded as she exited the admiral's office into the quiet hallway.

She smiled.

"Of course," she replied confidently, but didn't elaborate.

With that, she took his hand in hers, relieved to have gotten all of her concerns out in the open. A huge weight had been lifted off of her shoulders and she was ready to face the future with her new family.

Two weeks later…

"Where's Daddy?" A.J. glanced around the museum trying to find his father.

"I don't know, son," Kai sighed. "He was meant to meet us here over an hour ago."

All morning, Kai had felt nauseous and weak. Closing her eyes, she tried to hold back a flood tide of dizziness, but it wasn't working.

"Did he call you back yet?" her son asked.

She tried to smile but couldn't.

"Not yet."

"Maybe he's at another meeting?" A.J. frowned.

"Maybe," she gagged as another pang of nausea assaulted her.

Aiden had been attending more meetings and teaching workshops during the last few weeks, spending less and less time with them. On the off days he was home, he was locked away in his office working on lesson plans and reviewing professional journals and textbooks. Escaping his office only to eat, use the bathroom, or sleep. It was like living with a ghost.

"Let's finish up the museum tour and get some lunch."

"Can we eat at Monkey Burger?" A.J. requested as he licked his lips while rubbing his stomach.

"I guess so…" his mother wavered as the room started to spin.

"Mommy, are you ok?"

"Yes, I'm fine, but let's leave the rest of the tour for another day, okay?"

She felt sick, but she blamed it on missing her mid-morning snack. She'd been feeling worse each day for the last couple of days, throwing up even more than during her first trimester.

"Mommy?" A.J. held her hand sweetly as he examined her face. "You don't look very good…"

That was the last thing she heard before the room went black.

"Pardon me, ma'am," Aiden said, trying to get the charge nurse's attention.

His words a breathless rush as he recuperated from his recent sprint up three flights of stairs after deciding the elevator weren't moving fast enough.

"I'm looking for my wife… Mrs. Kai Kaplan," he frantically explained. "She was brought in a few hours ago from the Naval Museum."

The female nurse hit a few keys on her keyboard before speaking.

"Ah, yes...here she is." The nurse handed him a visitor's badge. "She's in room 305. Up the hall, make your first left, third door on the left."

"Thank you," he gasped before sprinting up the hallway to find Kai.

As he rounded the corner, he heard his father's deep baritone along with A.J.'s amused chuckle before he actually saw them. He quickened his pace, following the familiar voices until he found the right room. To his surprise, his father sat on a chair near the door, A.J. sitting on his lap, his very pale wife smiling at them both.

"...so, then the chicken said, 'you call that a knife, I'll show you a knife'," John said, mimicking a Swedish accent. Aiden remembered his dad telling him the same joke when he was a kid.

A.J. saw him first.

"Daddy, you're here!"

"Hi, son," he said as he shook his father's hand then bent to kiss A.J.'s forehead. "How's Mommy feeling?" He glanced in Kai's direction, but she looked down at her clenched fingers.

"I'm well," she answered dryly.

His father cleared his throat.

"Dr. Khan, the physician on duty when she arrived, said she's severely dehydrated," John updated him on his wife's wellbeing.

"Damn it!" He looked down at his son's shocked expression. "Sorry, I forgot. No swearing."

Aiden moved to sit on the edge of Kai's hospital bed. She still hadn't looked at him and it was making him nervous.

"They have her on an I.V. and her vitals are improving," John continued. "The baby is doing well, heartbeat's strong and healthy. They may want Kai to stay overnight to monitor her progress. Other than that, she's going to be just fine."

He released a breath he hadn't known he was holding.

"Thank God." He took Kai's hand in his even though she tried pulling it away.

"A.J.," his father spoke, distracting his grandson. "Let's go down to the cafeteria and get something to eat."

"Okay." He ran over and kissed his mom's cheek. "We'll be right back."

Her mouth lifted at the side, but she didn't smile.

"Kai, Aiden, would you like anything from the cafeteria?" John queried.

"Some Jell-O if they have any, and maybe some soup and crackers," Kai beamed. "I'm starving."

"No problem," his father replied. "Son?"

"Nothing for me, sir."

As soon as they left, he turned to face his wife.

"I'm so sorry," Aiden apologized. "I would have been here sooner if—"

"Where were you, Aiden?" Kai blurted. "The museum manager called your office and your cell phone. When he couldn't locate you, A.J. told him to call your dad. Thank God, John was between meetings and was in his office when they called. A.J. was so scared."

"What happened?"

"I guess I must have fainted," she confessed. "The lack of fluids in my system made me dizzy."

"I'm sorry." He kissed her knuckles. "Truly sorry, Kai. I should be taking better care of you. I've been busy with this teaching position. I didn't realize it would take up so much of my time. Between the prep-work and meetings—"

"Where were you?" she interrupted again.

"I had an emergency meeting with Commander Baker and my CO. My cell phone was charging in my office. I must have forgotten it. It wasn't until I got back to the office that I saw the missed calls."

"Why didn't you call to say you couldn't meet us at the museum?" she quizzed, eyes welling with tears.

"I forgot, I'm sorry," he babbled guiltily.

"You've been saying that a lot lately," she responded sarcastically. "Why don't you take A.J. home? I'm sure he's exhausted."

"I'll have my father take him to his place, so I can stay here with you."

"No," she said too quickly for his peace of mind. "I'll get more rest if I'm by myself."

"Kai—" he began but was cut off by her command.

"I want you to go home. I'll be fine. I'll see you tomorrow."

With that said, she closed her eyes.

"They want me to go to New Guinea next week," he said sheepishly. "I'll be gone for a little over two weeks…if everything goes well."

She didn't respond right away, and he felt his neck stiffen.

"Fine," she muttered under her breath.

"That's it?" he jabbed. "All you have to say is *fine*?"

She opened her eyes again, staring dead at him, eyes glistening with unshed tears.

"What would you like me to say, Kaplan?"

Shit!

"I don't know?" he blustered.

His wife continued to glare at him.

"If I begged and pleaded, would you stay with us?" she questioned.

"I can't," his voice was a bit raspy.

"Then there's nothing to say."

She closed her eyes once again and Aiden sat beside her until he heard the soothing sound of her soft snores.

It was obvious she didn't understand all of his hard work was going to provide their family with lots of opportunities. Aiden wanted to be able to give her the house of her dreams, pay for college for their children, take her on vacations around the world, and make a name for himself in the process.

Gently, he kissed her lips, amazed at how soft they were. He loved her more than he ever believed he could love anyone. All he could do was hope she felt the same about him. Whatever happened he needed her to stick by him during these difficult times.

One month later…

"A.J.," Kai called to her son, who was watching a cartoon on a local cable station in the living room. "Dinner is ready."

"What's for dinner?"

"Chicken pot pies," she announced, knowing it was one of his favorite foods.

"My favorite!" he sang as he ran into the kitchen, almost knocking her over in the process.

"Please walk before you get hurt," she gently admonished.

"Okay, Mommy."

Before he could sit, she requested asked him for a favor.

"Could you please let Daddy know the food is ready?"

"Okay."

On his mission, he ran off down the hallway returning soon after.

"Where's Daddy?" she asked, seeing him alone.

A.J. looked at her sadly.

"He said to eat without him. He's busy."

Kai sighed, her heart breaking a little more.

"Sweetie, please wash your hands. I'll be right back."

Steeling herself for the battle with her husband, she opened the door without knocking. Aiden looked up, blue eyes cloudy with fatigue.

"Dinner is ready," she informed with a hopeful smile. "Take a break and come eat with us."

"Sorry, baby, but I'm swamped," he groaned, reaching for his highlighter.

"It's chicken pot pie, piping hot," she informed, trying to lure him away from his pile of schematics.

Uninterested, he looked back down at the manual he was reading.

"I can't," he mumbled. "I really need to finish some research for a project I have to do at the end of the month."

He peeked up at her then glanced back down nervously.

"I'll be going to Florida for a couple of weeks."

"But you just got back," she whispered. "Okay, just come and eat with us...we miss you."

"Tomorrow, I promise."

Without another word, he resumed his research.

"When is Daddy coming home?"

"He was supposed to come home earlier this afternoon, but he hasn't called. I'm sure he's alright," she lied to her son, terrified at the thought of her husband in a ditch somewhere, bleeding out or something equally horrifying.

Pretending nothing was wrong, Kai read A.J. a story, waited for him to fall asleep, and then went to her room to take a shower. Trying to get her mind off of her husband, she read until eleven, drifting to sleep while waiting for Aiden to come home. At midnight, she heard the door open and a tall, shadowy figure entered the room, set his briefcase in the closet, and then stopped briefly to look down at her. She lay unmoving, pretending to be asleep, hoping he'd leave her alone. After a few seconds, he tiptoed to the bathroom closing the door behind him.

A few minutes later, she heard the shower turn on, then a few minutes after, it turned off. Nervously, she held her breath, staring longingly at the closed door until finally he exited the bathroom, a towel wrapped around his waist. She debated whether or not to acknowledge his presence but decided not to.

Even though she was so angry with him, she could spit, Kai had to admit he looked delicious. However, she still feigned sleep, even after he pressed his soft lips to her shoulder blade then snuggled against her back and fell asleep. She felt the first teardrop roll down her cheek, no longer able to hold it in as the emotional dam broke, releasing weeks of unshed tears.

CHAPTER THIRTEEN

One month later...

"Aiden," Kai stated, refusing to look at him. "This isn't working out."

The shakiness of her own voice alarmed her.

"What's not working out?" he frowned.

"This...*us*..." She waved her hand awkwardly between them.

Seemingly shocked, he gaped at her, running both hands through his wet hair.

"Yes, it is."

"Maybe for you," she tried steadying her breathing. "But it's not for me or our son."

Aiden sighed and sat back in his office chair.

"We all need to make adjustments—"

She shook her head fervidly, curly strands getting caught on her eyelashes.

"The only ones making adjustments are A.J. and me. We packed-up and left everything we know, everyone we love... *for you*... to be a family," she whimpered.

"Exactly, we are a family," his voice rose. "We're meant to stick together. No matter what."

Without another word, Kai turned and walked out of his home office and back to their bedroom, hastily shedding her blue flannel robe and snuggling under the covers. Aiden already showered and dressed for bed, wearing only loose-fitting striped pajama bottoms that hung sexily off his waist, sat beside her on the bed, looking lost.

"Aiden." She tugged his wrist making him lay next to her. "Your intentions are noble. They really are. And I think you love the idea of having a family, but without all of the complications that come with it."

"That's not true," he denied with a pained expression. "I know what it takes to hold a family together."

"No, you don't," she reprimanded. "You're doing to us what your father did to you after your mother died. You leave us alone for weeks at a time while you go traipsing around the world knowing A.J. and I are here... alone... waiting for you to come back home. Then when you're with us, you're not really with us."

"That's not true," he replied again.

"Most times you're either at meetings or conferences or formal functions and when you are here, you spend most of your time in your office. Then when you finally do come out of your office, A.J. and I are already asleep," she ranted like a mad person.

"I've been busy with work, Kai," he stressed. "I'm trying to give—"

"Remember when you promised to show us around the museum then didn't even show up or call to say you couldn't make it and it was your idea to go there in the first place," she continued as though he hadn't said anything.

He shook his head.

"I already apologized for that."

She sighed, the sound full of anguish and frustration.

"I know you did, but you also promised to spend more time with your son, and you haven't done that either."

"Kai, it's not just me anymore," he growled. "I've got you and A.J. to provide for and I still have dreams of my own too—"

"There. You. Go," her voice climbed an octave. "It's always about you. Like you said, Aiden, it's not just you anymore. You are now part of a *We*. We...meaning not an island unto yourself anymore. I have dreams of my own, like furthering my education, maybe owning my own home...having another little one in a few years."

She stared at him, her cheeks flushed, eyes glistening in the brightly lit room.

"But I was willing to put my dreams on the back burner for us...for you."

"I don't understand," he rambled. "I thought everything was going well. Now you throw this at me."

"Are you serious?!" Kai snapped.

"Extremely serious," he said with annoyance. "A long time ago, you convinced me not to rely on my father for anything, remember? Not to use his money, to become self-reliant, a better person. Well, that's what I'm trying to do."

"So," her voice rose. "This is my fault?"

"That's not what I said," he huffed.

"Yes, you did," she accused.

"Listen," Aiden spoke without heat. "I want to give you everything you deserve. A nice car, a beautiful house, vacations around the world. I want to give you the world."

"But I don't want the world. I just want you." She began crying, unable to control the flow. "It's always been you, Aiden. I've only ever loved you."

"You should have told me how you felt," he spewed indignantly. "How was I to know you were unhappy?"

"Sonofabitch!" She punched him on the shoulder as hard as she could. "You couldn't tell I was unhappy...that A.J. was miserable...that he missed

spending time with you? When was the last time you tucked him into bed or read him a bedtime story?"

He glared at her, anger and disappointment creating harsh lines across his forehead.

"I've been busy, Kai."

"Yeah, you've been busy with everyone except us, your family."

Kai couldn't contain her rage any longer, the tiny tear molecules tickling her warm skin only pushed her further over the emotional cliff. She took in a shuddering breath then slowly released it like a balloon stuck by a sharp instrument, air flowing out in a rush.

"I'm taking A.J. back to Oahu," she told with a monotonous tone. "School starts in two weeks, the day after Labor Day, and I need to get him enrolled. We only have our clothes and a few new things that can go back with us in the suitcases. Anything that doesn't fit you can ship to us."

For a long time, he sat reviewing the finality of her words.

"Where will you live?" his voice strained with disbelief. "How will you work while taking care of two kids?"

"We'll move back in with my parents," she sniffled. "They've got plenty of room. As for work, I left on good terms with my supervisor. I'm sure I can get my old job back without a problem."

He sat for a moment, silently mulling over her answers. His jaw clenched and his fists curled so tightly his knuckles were turning white.

"What about A.J.?" he grimaced. "Are you going to let me see him?"

"Of course, I'd never stop you from seeing your son," she reassured. "I love…he loves you very much. You can visit anytime. He can visit you in the summers and during spring break and long holidays."

"It's not the same and you know it," he harrumphed angrily, and Kai was suddenly frightened.

"I won't stand in the way of your relationship with your son," she promised. "He needs to have you in his life."

Suddenly, he bolted off the bed, pacing like a caged lion, eyes so dark they appeared black.

"Stop being so damn considerate and matter-of-fact about this, don't you give a shit?"

"Believe me, I'm trying my hardest not to have a nervous breakdown," her voice wavered.

"What about the baby?" he glanced away then back.

"Same rules apply," Kai whispered. "Of course, you'll have to wait until she's older, but you can visit anytime."

"I don't want to visit; I just want all of us to be together!" he hissed through clenched teeth.

"Are you ready to just do the teaching position?" she countered.

"No," he tossed back.

"What about transferring permanently to Pearl Harbor-Hickam like we originally discussed? What about that? Then you'd only be gone for special projects and the kids, and I will have family close by to help out. Here we have no support system, and I can't do this by myself, Aiden. I *won't* do this by myself."

"That's unfair," he hissed.

"What's unfair about asking you to compromise? I did. I'm here, with you, instead of with my family who I miss terribly. It feels like someone ripped my heart out I miss them so badly."

"Don't do this. Don't give up on me." He was trembling with rage.

"I've tried," she calmed herself. "I'm not saying I don't love you. I love you so much it hurts to breathe, but you've left me with no other choice," she admitted through uncontrolled sobs.

"If I box myself into one category it will take me longer to get promotions," he replied, finally looking directly into her watery, amber eyes.

"And there it is." She sat up, her hands instinctively covering her now much larger belly. "You choose your career over your family because you have something to prove to your father."

He didn't say anything, just watched her movements, his cheeks flushed.

"At least your dad has changed," she mumbled.

"What are you talking about?"

"I forgot… you haven't been around for me to catch you up on our daily drama," she replied more calmly. "After the incident at the museum, when your dad was with me at the hospital… he apologized for everything. He said he was an ass for not telling you about the pregnancy… about not coming to the wedding… and for all the awful things he said to me."

"What did he say to you?"

She smiled.

"It doesn't matter. John and I are in a good place now."

"That's impossible," he stated in a firm tone. "My dad doesn't apologize for anything."

"He must be softening in his old age," Kai supposed.

Aiden's arms folded across his chest in a show of defiance.

"I don't believe it."

"Do you know your dad comes to visit us every couple of days? He and A.J. have a great time together. He's teaching him how to fish. The last time they went out they caught a three-pound striped bass. A few weeks ago, he took us out to the amusement park. A.J. got to ride on his first roller coaster. I guess he's tall for his age. And next week, they were supposed to be going on a working aircraft carrier… just like he did with you when you were his age."

"I'll be damned," Aiden whispered. "I guess old dogs can learn new tricks."

"Your father has been there for us more than you have," she added, her hackles rising once again.

"What do you want me to do?" He stopped in his tracks, his back to her. "Quit the Navy?"

"No, never. I just want you to choose us," she frowned. "Who cares if your promotions slowdown a little? I certainly won't judge you any differently whether you're a lieutenant or an admiral. I just care that you're with us. Please, pick one…teacher or working engineer. What's it gonna be, Kaplan?"

He was silent for a long, tension-filled moment.

"I can't do that."

Kai heard a gasp rip out of her lungs and she felt as if he'd physically struck her, even though he was several feet away.

"I'll go sleep on the couch," he said with an air of insolence, turning toward the door.

She stood ram-rod straight.

"I won't wait another decade for you, Kaplan," she educated bluntly. "I deserve better than to sit around hoping you come to your senses. I want a man who's willing to put his family before anything else."

His cheeks reddened.

"You want a divorce?"

"That's the only course you've left me." She wiped away a tear. "It doesn't have to be right away, at least not until after the baby is born."

"I thought you loved me, Kai."

"I do, you know I do," she stated. "But I'm not going to play second fiddle to your career for the next fifty years."

He didn't respond as he walked mechanically to the door, leaving her alone with her misery.

Two days later...

"Here's the cell phone I got for you. We can send text messages and talk to each other at any time." Aiden hugged his son tightly, not caring that A.J. was wiggling in his arms.

"Daddy," he gasped for breath, "I can't breathe." Reluctantly, he released him, staring at his face trying to memorize every detail.

"Remember to charge it every night before you go to sleep."

"I will," A.J. replied his words drenched with sadness.

"Good." Aiden stood. "Don't forget you've got to help take care of the baby and Mommy."

He still couldn't believe this was happening. The brilliant, Hawaiian bombshell he had loved since he was nineteen was leaving him. The need to beg became a living entity floating around his brain, but he ignored it.

"Yes, sir."

"Good boy," Aiden felt his chest tighten.

"When will you visit? Will it be soon?" A.J. grilled.

"I'm hoping to visit for Thanksgiving," he stated confidently.

"Cool!"

"Maybe Christmas too," Aiden added, glancing at his son's mother.

"You can stay at our house."

Aiden glanced at his wife longingly.

"We'll see, buddy."

He heard Kai's sigh.

"Come on, A.J. We've got to go," she hurried him along. "We don't want to miss our flight to Honolulu."

"I love you, Daddy." His little boy hugged him around the waist.

Aiden's chest tensed again.

"I love you too, little man."

"I'll let him call when we reach home." Kai wouldn't look at him. "Let's go, A.J."

Determined not to change her mind, she held their son's small hand, grabbed her carryon, and started heading toward the gate. Their plane was almost finished boarding and they had to get on now or miss the flight. He watched her walk away, hips swaying in that sexy way of hers, curls pulled back into a high ponytail and no make-up…and she was still gorgeous. He shook his head wondering how she could make a simple pair of maternity jeans and t-shirt look so damn good.

"Kai, wait!" he shouted, running to reach her, and pulled her into his arms, burying his nose in her jasmine-scented hair. "Please, don't go. Don't leave. We can get through this. I know we can."

He felt when her arms wrapped around his waist and her body relaxed.

"Then you've picked one."

"Be reasonable," he begged.

She stiffened again then pulled away tiptoeing to reach his mouth. Her lips were so soft, so full, and when she kissed him with a desperate passion that made his legs shake, he understood it would be the last time he would ever kiss her.

"I love you," she whispered so only he could hear, and then holding A.J.'s hand walked to the check-in desk and disappeared down the corridor. Leaving him standing in the middle of the airport.

Alone.

There was a knock on the door waking Aiden from a fitful sleep. Blinking, he tried to concentrate, his vision blurry with exhaustion. Slowly, his eyes focused enough to make out the time on the Blue-Ray's digital display. It was a little past midnight, and he was pissed.

Another anxious knock came again, and he wondered if he should ignore it.

"Wait a minute, damn it! I'm coming!" he yelled, not caring if he woke the neighbors. Fuck everybody.

He threw open the door, surprised at who was waiting on the other side wearing a pair of jeans and a red polo with a Navy crest on it.

"What the hell do you want?"

He turned back to where he was sleeping on the couch. He hadn't slept in his bedroom in over a week. It smelled of jasmine and Kai. Carelessly, he dropped onto the leather causing the springs to squeak in complaint.

"I'm not in the mood for your shit, so just turn back around and get out," he growled.

John Kaplan stepped inside closing the door firmly behind him.

"Wallowing in self-pity working out for you, son?"

"Shut up, old man." Aiden glared at his father, his face looking a bit sallow in the dark room.

"Why haven't you been to work in over a week?"

"I've been sick," he lied.

"Sure." John sat on the matching recliner watching him. "I spoke with Kai and A.J. today. She told me a little about what happened between the two of you. You really fucked-up, Aiden."

Aiden sat up, blinked, then opened his mouth to say something, but decided against it.

"Kai's the best thing that's happened to you. I've never seen you happier or crazier than when you were with her." John chuckled knowingly. "Remember when you first met her and she dropped that book on your head and you called me to complain."

"Yes." Aiden smiled remembering the large knot she had made on his head.

"I knew you were a goner even then," the admiral cleared his throat. "Did I ever tell you how your mom and I met?"

Aiden shook his head.

"I had recently started graduate school and I was at the local library doing research for a paper and couldn't locate the reference book I needed. She was the librarian on duty that day: tall, beautiful, very prim and proper. I complained about not finding the book and accused her of not doing her job."

"Why did you do that?" he managed a slight grin.

"Because she made me nervous and I wanted to gain the upper hand," John chuckled.

"Did it work?" Aiden prodded. "Did she lose her cool?"

"Sort of," his father snickered. "She walked with me back to the reference section and found the book where she said it would be. Apparently, I was looking for it on the wrong shelf. I remember telling her she was too smug and uptight."

Aiden sat up enjoying his father's story.

"Then what happened?"

"She dropped the five-pound quantum mechanics book I was looking for, on my foot, on purpose. Then turned and walked away without even an apology."

Aiden laughed.

"I went back to that library every day for a month trying to get her to go out with me," his father smirked at the memory. "Finally, she broke down when I threatened to start a fire in the historical section."

"Damn!" Aiden shook his head and belly laughed for the first time in a week. "That's pretty pathetic, Dad."

"Yes, but it was worth it," his father replied sadly. "I had fifteen amazing years with her before the car accident and I wouldn't change a moment of it."

John paused briefly.

"I really fucked up with you, Aiden."

He stood and walked over to admire the pictures on Aiden's shelving unit. Briefly, he stopped at the picture of him and Kai on their wedding day, and then turned to another photo of A.J. playing basketball.

"When your mother died my whole world stopped and never restarted, and every time I looked at you...I saw...her," he sighed before he continued. "Her smile, her sense of humor, her ability to make fun of herself and oftentimes me, I saw all those qualities in you. And it broke my heart a little more every day. So, I threw myself into my career and never looked back."

"You were a right bastard for doing that," Aiden said unsympathetically.

"I never realized I was," John ignored his hurtful remark. "It wasn't until your wife told me off that it really hit me what an idiot I've been."

"She did that?" Aiden's chest filled with pride. "She never told me what happened in your office after I left...fearless minx."

"Kai is an amazing person," his dad smirked. "Smart, beautiful, caring, and she doesn't take crap from anyone. She reminds me of your mother."

Aiden smiled again.

"She does, doesn't she?"

"Fix this, son," his father encouraged. "Go get your family back before it's too late."

John stood to leave.

"I... I love you, Aiden," John professed. "Always have, always will, but if you let Kai slip away... I'll disinherit you then kick your stubborn ass."

Aiden grinned.

"Sir, yes sir." He looked at the older man in a new light. "But I'll need your help. I know I shouldn't try to gain by using your position, but—"

"Aiden, anything you need, just let me know," John reassured with a smile.

"Suppose she won't take me back?" he scowled. "She's stubborn, even more than mom."

"Grow some stones, my boy," his father bristled. "You are a Kaplan. You can do anything you set your mind to." John cleared his throat. "I'm proud of the man you've become. I know your mom would be proud of you too."

"Thanks."

"You're welcome," the older version of him blushed. "Now, figure out a way to fix this situation."

Rubbing the nape of his neck nervously, he mumbled, "I don't know how—"

His dad's eyebrow arched.

"Are you afraid of her son?"

"A little bit," he chuckled. "She can be ruthless and the mouth on her, don't get me started."

His father gave him a mock salute.

"Fix it," he commanded. "Before you end up like me, old and miserable."

"Dad." Aiden walked over to the fridge. "You wanna a beer?"

CHAPTER FOURTEEN

"How are you feeling, sweetie?"

"Nauseous," Kai replied with a mouth stuffed with Saltines.

Two months without Aiden was pure, unadulterated torture, and with the pregnancy progressing she was always tired.

She couldn't sleep without Aiden beside her. The bed seemed empty without him in it. She hadn't spoken to her husband since they left Annapolis, but A.J. spoke to Aiden every night via video chat. It wasn't the same though. He promised A.J. to visit for Thanksgiving and *she* couldn't wait.

Evelyn watched her cautiously.

"What's the matter?"

"A.J. misses him a lot," she stated sadly, tears threatened to fall again. "But he's a tough little guy."

Evelyn patted her sympathetically.

"No more crying," her friend encouraged. "You'll make me want to cry too."

"I miss him too," Kai sniffled.

"I know you do, sweetie." Evelyn put her hands on her plump hips and started tapping her foot. "You want me to find that boy and kick his very firm, tasty ass?"

Kai giggled.

"No, please don't."

"Let me know if you change your mind," the nurse winked.

"I will," she grumbled. "Evelyn?"

"Yes?"

"I think I made a mistake leaving him," Kai admitted as she sniffled once more.

"Try not to think about it," her longtime confidant encouraged. "Why don't you take your break? You could use some time to yourself. I'll let the receptionist at the PT desk know where you are."

Too exhausted to argue, Kai nodded then headed toward the physical therapy employee break room. She felt more depressed with every passing day. Suddenly, a loud screech came from the overhead speaker system.

"Kai Kaplan," a muffled male voice came through the speaker. "Paging, Mrs. Kai Kapahu-Kaplan... *Damn it*, are you sure this thing is working?"

A female voice quickly followed over the loud-speaker.

"Yes, sir, it works just fine and please watch your language."

"Shit! Hell! I'm sorry...! Kai, please report to the reception desk in the front lobby... STAT. I've always wanted to say that."

The receptionist's voice could be heard again in the background.

"Please, sir, give me back the microphone or I'll call security—"

Kai speed-walked to the front lobby as fast as her almost full-term belly would allow. She didn't know what the hell was going on, but she was going to find out.

Thank goodness she made it to the lobby without injury.

"Tina, what the hell is going on?" she asked the pretty blonde receptionist.

From behind her, she heard the sound of music... loud and very... disco-ish.

Holy shit! Was she dreaming?

Turning around, she spotted him. Tall, devilishly handsome and dressed in an exact replica of John Travolta's disco suit in the movie *Saturday Night Fever* and also sporting a rather large, dark afro.

Oh, no, no, no!

Not here, not now.

Before she could stop her obviously insane husband, he began to sing along to the karaoke version of *You're Every Woman in the World*, loud, out of tune and too sexy for words.

"If you don't want him back, I'll take him." Evelyn appeared beside her, grinning from ear to ear.

When Aiden finished the entire song, he bowed to the thunderous applause and then stalked over to where she was standing, picked her up in his arms and kissed her until she couldn't speak.

"I love you, Kai," he winked playfully. "Always have always will. Now, let's get out of here."

"Aiden, stop, what about Annapolis?" she grilled, holding on for dear life.

"My father pulled a few strings and I'll be stationed permanently at Pearl as the lead engineer on base...only traveling when absolutely necessary," he beamed.

"What about your townhouse in Maryland?" she huffed.

He kissed her gently this time.

"I sold it to a buddy of mine who's been eyeing it for a while."

"You won't be able to see Marcus...or your dad—"

"I can talk to Marcus via Zoom anytime and we can visit him and Vanessa and the baby during summers, or they can visit us here," he educated gleefully.

"What about your father?" she questioned with her hands perched on her hips.

Aiden smiled the crooked boy-next-door-smile and she melted.

"Dad is coming for a visit after the baby is born. The old man misses his grandson like crazy, and his daughter-in-law. Did he tell you he has our wedding picture on his desk?"

She nodded.

"He also has one of A.J. and him with that huge bass they caught a few months ago. He's got a copy of one of your sonograms of Peanut too."

Kai shook her head again, everything he said sounding too good to be true.

"You won't be happy just being a family man, Aiden."

"While you were gone, I realized being a family man is the only thing I do need," he confessed.

"You're only saying that to—"

He cut her off in midsentence.

"Kai, I want to be with you," he stated boldly. "I want to play volleyball on Sundays with you. I want to argue with you about what movies we want to see at the theatre. I want to raise beautiful babies with you."

"Ok," she giggled. "I get the point, Madman."

"I love you, Amazon."

"I love you too—" A gush of warm fluid rushed out of her core, trickling down her inner thighs and her eyes widened in disbelief. "Oh...no...Aiden."

"What the... What's the matter? Why am I wet?" Aiden looked as if he was about to faint.

"I think my water just broke!" she yelped with surprise.

He blinked once...twice...

"Say that again."

"I'm having the baby now!" she hissed.

"Right now?!"

"Aiden, focus, our baby is ready to come out now."

"But you're not due yet!" he bellowed. "You're early...oh, man you can't be early. Do we even have a crib?"

Kai smiled despite his panic.

"The PT staff along with Evelyn gave me a baby shower last month and my family had one for me this past weekend."

"Don't panic, Daddy," Evelyn interrupted, smiling reassuringly. "I'll take over from here. Follow me young man, I'll show you where to change into some scrubs. Tina, call labor and delivery and tell them I need a delivery room for Kai, thanks, sweetie. Call Dr. Sung, he's in the doctor's lounge and tell him she's ready to deliver. Kai, slow deep breaths, remember? It's like riding a bike."

The nurse gave him a saucy wink.

"Let's go, Lieutenant Kaplan. You're gonna be a daddy, again."

EPILOGUE

Six weeks later…

"Where are we going, Aiden?" Kai stared out of the window at the familiar scenery. "Are we going to my parents' house?"

"You'll see." He couldn't help but laugh at her. "Why can't you ever be—"

"I know, I know: be patient." She rolled her eyes at him.

A few minutes later, he pulled their brand new, black mini-van up to the entrance of the Kona Cove gated community. The same subdivision where his wife's parents lived. It was an impressive development with well-maintained homes and yards. Spectacular views of Koko Crater, an elementary school located less than a mile away and several playgrounds sprinkled throughout the subdivision. He also liked it because there were only one hundred homes in the community with a mixture of young families and older retired couples. It was perfect for them.

He punched the code into the gate then waited patiently as it opened.

"You okay back there, A.J.?" Aiden asked his son who was sitting quietly in the back seat.

"Yes, Daddy." He smiled. "Aria is still sleeping."

A.J. touched his six-week-old baby sister gently on the cheek.

"Aiden," Kai gasped. "You took the wrong turn. My parents live two streets down, remember?"

"I know," he chuckled.

A few minutes later, he found the wrap-around driveway to a two-story contemporary home with large palladium windows at the end of the cul-de-sac. Kai's breath hitched and he smiled to himself. His wife turned to face him, amber eyes glistening in the bright mid-morning sunshine.

"What did you do?"

"I'm checking off one of the items on your wish list."

He leaned across the console holding her chin in place.

"Welcome home, baby," he said, enjoying his wife's speechlessness. "I hope you like it."

Getting out of the car, he helped A.J. with his seatbelt, before taking his newborn daughter's car carrier out of the secured base. They wandered around the beautifully manicured front yard examining all of the hibiscus bushes, multi-colored flowerbeds, various fruit trees, and low, neatly shaped hedges.

"We can put a swing set in the backyard since it's already fenced," Aiden stated proudly.

"How could you afford to buy this?" Kai looked like she was about to faint.

"I used the money from the sale of my townhouse in Annapolis, plus a little extra from my savings. Our parents helped too… my dad included."

"No, way," she mumbled, eyes tearing.

"Here you are, Mrs. Kaplan." Aiden put the key to the house in her hand. "Let's check out inside."

On cloud nine, Kai led the way to the front door of the house. Her hand shook a little as she inserted the key into the newly changed lock. He realized he was holding his breath, anticipation choking him.

"Hurry," he encouraged. "You're killing me, Kai."

"Stop rushing me," she pouted. "You're making me even more nervous."

"Sorry, hurry up!" he rushed, poking her in the leg with Aria's carrier.

"Mommy, you're taking too long," A.J. chimed in.

Aiden tried unsuccessfully to stifle his laughter. Kai shot him her patented look of death, which only made him laugh louder.

"I didn't say anything." He placed Aria's carrier seat between him and his now seething wife. "Okay, baby, please…unlock the door."

Finally, she got the door open, slowly stepping inside while he and their son followed. Aiden took the opportunity to ogle her ass. The dark washed Bermuda shorts hugging her curves deliciously.

"Stop staring at my butt," Kai scolded omnisciently. "It's inappropriate."

"Since when," he questioned, arching a brow in her direction, curious to hear her answer.

Kai narrowed her eyes.

"Since we're married with children," she reminded with confidence.

"If I'd never ogled your butt, we wouldn't be married with children," he countered with a smirk.

"Pig," she hissed.

"You are insane," he informed his grinning wife then snorted loudly.

"Why am I insane?" she blustered.

"Could you please get out of the way, Aria and I are coming in."

Gently, he placed his hand at the small of her back, and then led her into the foyer. He heard her swallow hard, whispering in Hawaiian under her breath.

Filled with excitement, she grabbed his wrist closest to her and squeezed.

"It's gorgeous!" she squealed. "I knew you had good taste. After all, you fell in love with me."

She waggled her brows.

"But this is unbelievable!"

"Let's take a look around." He held her hand leading her through each room.

The house was similar to Leilani and Joseph's with cathedral ceilings, built-in entertainment centers and shelving systems in the formal and informal living rooms, and tons of windows allowing lots of natural light.

"Amazing!" she glowed, touching the hand carved banister like it would disappear if she stopped.

"You've got to take a look at the kitchen," he beckoned animatedly. Kai followed him closely, a large, toothy smile pasted on her face. "It truly is amazing, isn't it?"

"It really is. Emeril will be jealous," she teased.

And it was amazing.

Aiden loved the completely remodeled, gourmet kitchen with granite countertops, dark-stained solid wood cabinets and brand-new stainless-steel appliances including a custom wine fridge. His favorite features of the area; however, were the impressive double farmhouse sinks and separate kitchen island with extra cabinet space and mini-sink. On the far side of the room was a built-in computer console/desk with shelves like at his townhouse along with a breakfast nook overlooking the lanai.

Kai giggled as she gazed out of the large kitchen window.

"The view of Koko Crater is incredible."

"No time to dawdle." He tugged her along. "We've gotta see the backyard. I think A.J.'s already out there."

When Kai opened the French doors leading to the huge backyard, she was greeted with thunderous applause, deafening cat calls, and hoots and hollers.

Claiming Kai

The entire Kapahu family was out in the yard along with picnic tables filled with food and temporary folding chairs.

"What's going on?" Kai studied her husband, who was grinning from ear to ear.

Her father waved at her from the grill.

"It's Sunday and we're getting ready to eat brunch."

The delicious aroma of grilling meat made her stomach growl.

"Mommy, there's even a volleyball net set up!" her son announced while dancing around her feet.

Aiden handed Aria, who was still asleep in her carrier, to her Uncle Koa, who had just stepped up beside them.

"A.J. stay here. I'm gonna show Mommy upstairs."

"Okay." Their little boy ran off to play with the other kids.

"Koa, are you okay with the baby?" Aiden asked, looking a bit anxious about leaving his baby girl.

Koa chuckled.

"No worries, *braddah*. I've got lots of practice taking care of little ones."

Taking her husband's hand, Kai was given the tour of the other rooms downstairs which included an office with built-in bookshelves, laundry room with sink and storage area, formal dining room and family room, and a three-car garage.

"This is just like Mama and Papa's house." She couldn't help the astonishment in her voice.

"There's more," he revealed, blue eyes gleaming.

Her husband led her upstairs, showing her all four bedrooms starting with the smaller rooms first.

"I figured A.J. can have the largest of the bedrooms since he's the oldest."

She nodded in agreement.

"We'll put Aria in the bedroom closest to us until she's a little older," Kai informed, busy decorating each of the rooms in her mind.

"And here is the master bedroom," Aiden announced as they entered the enormous master bedroom with ensuite bathroom.

She looked around in awe, breathing heavy, mouth slightly ajar.

"Do you like it?" he poked.

"It's what I've always wanted," she confirmed with gusto.

Aiden waggled his eyebrows.

"The bathroom has a separate shower and a Jacuzzi tub big enough for at least four people."

"Deviant," she whispered.

"Prude," he grinned.

Leaving him temporarily, Kai jogged into the adjoining room and called to him.

"We've got double-sinks and our own linen closet. My goodness! There are his and hers walk-in closets too. Holy crap!"

Aiden followed her into the largest closet where she stood admiring the built-in, custom storage unit.

"I could live in here," she muttered under her breath.

Aiden chuckled enjoying her excitement.

"I'm assuming you like it."

"I love it, Aiden!" she purred happily. "This is perfect, simply perfect."

"It's all for you."

"I know," she purred again, pulling him against her body, chest to chest.

She still hadn't lost all of her pregnancy weight, but the way Aiden looked at her she knew he still found her sexy. During the past six weeks, they were instructed by her doctor not to have sex, which was fine with her. After all, she'd gone six years without sex, but Aiden was having a hard time. No pun intended.

"You know," she began, and kissed the sides of his mouth enjoying the way he tasted. "We need to christen these rooms."

"Kai," he whispered, mortified at the idea of someone walking in on them... *doing the do*. "We can't have sex now. Your entire family is waiting for us downstairs."

"So," she hinted wryly, batting her eyelashes. not caring who was downstairs. Seductively, she kissed the sensitive spot right below his left ear, encouraged when he released a soft moan. However, his hands were clenched at his sides refusing to touch her.

"This is not a good idea," he whispered, arching his neck to give her better access.

With deft fingers, Kai unbuttoned his shirt and kissed a trail from his collarbone to his left nipple. She greeted the flat surface with a quick flick with the tip of her tongue. A groan escaped him before he could rein it back in.

"Well, if you can't handle the challenge, I'll understand." She gave his nipple another wet glide. Angling her head so he could smell the jasmine shampoo she knew he loved.

"Really," he stated firmly, arching against her. "I can *handle* the challenge."

"I wouldn't want you to do anything you don't want to," she chuckled, feigning innocence. "I'll take care of it myself."

Aiden's brow arched at her odd answer.

"What do you mean by *'take care of it myself'*?"

"I bought one of those things...you know...a *pocket rocket*, but I haven't tested it yet," she admitted slyly.

"Dear God," he muttered.

She knew she had won when she felt his erection on her hip and smiled to herself.

"You *wouldn't* dare?"

"But I *would* dare," she announced casually. "It's right here in my purse."

"I don't think this is a good idea," her husband muttered half-heartedly, his willpower rapidly fading like a whisper in a windstorm.

"Don't worry about it, honey," she giggled. "It'll just take me a few minutes to work out my *kinks*."

Blue eyes narrowed suspiciously.

"Since when do you have *kinks*?" he interrogated.

"Since a very handsome, very sexy, very determined man *ruined* me."

Kai turned to walk away but didn't get more than a couple of feet away from her incredible *GQ* model of a husband, before Aiden grabbed her around the waist.

He growled seductively as he commanded, "Come here, woman."

HAWAIIAN PRONUNCIATIONS

Ali'ikai - *[ah lee 'ee kai]*; King or Queen of the Sea

Aloha - *[ah low ha]*; Love, affection; greeting, salutation; Hello! Good-bye!

Aloha au ia 'oe – I love you.

Haole – *[how lee]*; A foreigner; Pidgin slang – Caucasian

Kapahu – *[kah pah who]*

Koa - *[koh' (w)ah]*; Brave, Bold, Fearless

Kolohe – *[koh' low hee]*; Rascal

Shaka – A hand gesture which is most commonly used to convey the aloha spirit as a motion or greeting of thanks.

Leilani - *[lay lah nee]*; Heavenly Lei; Royal Child

Mahalo – Thank you.

ABOUT THE AUTHOR

L. D. K. Johnson is an American author hailing from the East Coast of the U.S., where she enjoys spending time with family and friends when she is not sitting in front of her laptop writing the next book that comes to mind.

Her favorite things in life are chocolate, creamer [not necessarily coffee], and anything D.I.Y. related.

Family is everything.

COMING SOON

By L.D.K. Johnson

SEALing the Deal

Episode #2 of The Kapahu Series

(Dun-dun-dun-dunnn)

And

COUNTING STARS

A Novel

CPSIA information can be obtained
at www.ICGtesting.com
Printed in the USA
BVHW061000240223
659164BV00003B/373